Happiland

Happiland

WILLIAM BEDFORD

HEINEMANN : LONDON

William Heinemann Ltd
Michelin House, 81 Fulham Road, London SW3 6RB
LONDON   MELBOURNE   AUCKLAND

First published 1990
Copyright © William Bedford 1990

British Library Cataloguing in Publication Data

Bedford, William
I. Title
823′.914[F]

ISBN 0 434 05559 X

Acknowledgements are due to the editors of *London Magazine*
and the *Malahat Review* where sections of this novel,
in a different form, originally appeared.

Printed in Great Britain by
St Edmundsbury Press Limited, Bury St Edmunds, Suffolk

For Fiona, Rachael and Thomas

One

When his work was finished, Harry went down to the promenade and sat at one of the window tables in Brown's café. From the window, he could see the pier and the deserted shores, and the slipway where the inshore fishing boats would come when the tide began to ebb. Great banks of cloud were gathering at the estuary, and as he ordered a mug of scalding hot tea and a bacon buttie with onions, the wind howled and gusted along the promenade, whistling underneath the café door. He fed some sixpences into the juke box, selecting Rosemary Clooney and Tennessee Ernie Ford, Frankie Laine and Teresa Brewer, and then sat down to wait for his food. He had spent all day baiting the fishing lines with frozen bait, and now he was waiting for George Bainbridge to get back from his trip to see what fresh lugworms were required tomorrow. During the winter months, when the fairgrounds were closed, Harry's only money came from the casual bait digging he did for the inshore fishermen. In the summer, he worked on the fairgrounds.

The café was empty until gone four, when Herbert Edlin came in noisily, slamming the door behind him and blowing on his hands.

'Mug of tea please, Peter,' he shouted to Brown, and sat down opposite Harry, unfastening his duffel coat and rubbing his hands together vigorously.

'Christ, don't look so cheerful, lad. Wait till you've got rheumatism like mine.'

'I think I already have,' Harry grinned, flexing his fingers which were still white from handling the cold worms.

'You don't know what the word means, lad,' Herbert said firmly, and continued blowing on his fingers.

Herbert was one of the oldest bait diggers on the East Coast. He'd worked with Harry's grandfather on the distant-water trawlers during the twenties and thirties, but had been on the bait digging since the Second World War. He said it was easier money. The only thing he didn't like about the job was baiting the snoods. The professional fishermen used dead bait, rolled into coils and wrapped up in old newspaper and then frozen. It was better than putting the live worms on to the hooks, but your hands got red raw after a couple of hours. Herbert blew noisily on his fingers, and when Brown brought the tea, held the mug between both hands.

'Nowt like a mug of hot tea,' he sighed. 'Can't say owt for the taste, mind. Never make it strong enough, these incomers.'

'Watch yourself, Herbert,' Brown threatened.

'Only been here five minutes.' Herbert winked at Harry. 'Not like me and your grandfather. He knew how to make a cup of tea.'

'He still does,' Harry laughed.

'Bag of tea, bag of sugar, and a tin of Carnation cream. That's what you want, Peter. Sling the lot into water and boil. Stand a shovel in Jack's tea, you could. I've known men die of tea fever after bunking with Jack Ellis.'

'I'll offer him a job,' Brown grinned.

'He wouldn't work with you,' Herbert said solemnly. 'How long is it you say you've been in this town?'

'Eighteen years.'

'Christ,' Herbert muttered. 'No wonder your tea's so weak.'

Harry finished his bacon buttie and lit a cigarette.

On a good day's digging, Herbert might get five hundred worms. Huge digs of a thousand and over were exceptional, but Herbert got them if anybody did. Supplying the local fishermen, he could earn a couple of quid a day during the winter, and more in the summer months when trippers didn't know what they were paying. Only the trippers used the bait

live, and Herbert despised them. He'd taught Harry everything he needed to know to make a decent living, and still
had secrets he wouldn't begin to discuss.

'How's it going, Herbert?' Harry asked now. 'Finished for
the day?'

'Allus see the boats back,' Herbert said. 'Get tomorrow's
order.'

'You want some more tea?'

'If you can call it tea.'

As Harry went up to the counter to get two fresh mugs,
the door opened and Arthur came into the café. A gust of
wind slammed the door back against a table, and he grabbed
for the handle, cursing loudly. Inside, he clapped his hands
and thumped Herbert hard on the back.

'Bunking off again, Herbert?'

'You cheeky bugger.'

'No offence. Christ, that wind. Going to be rough, I
reckon. Cup of tea please, Peter.'

'You got any money?'

'Course I have. Sold a lovely bit of fish this afternoon. Get
us a mug, Harry. Biggest cod I've ever seen.'

'That won't be saying much, then,' Herbert grumbled,
massaging his shoulder.

'Now, now, Herbert.'

'Stolen, was it?' Harry grinned, giving Arthur the lead he
knew he wanted.

'Naturally.'

'I don't know how you kids get away with it,' Brown
complained, 'the security they've got down those docks these
days.'

'Bacon buttie with it please, Peter. I thought I've got to
have her. Lumpers put a few aside in a basket, you know.
Backhanders. Green scales, lovely eyes, straight from the
bottom of the sea. Bit like Dickie Valentine. So I took her.
Derek Grant give me five shillings.'

'He's another fly bugger, 'n' all,' Brown grunted.

'You can't say that about Mr Universe,' Harry laughed. 'He'll break your neck.'

'How'd you get it off the docks then, this fish?' Brown asked sceptically, wiping the top of the counter and putting some fresh bacon on to the grill for Arthur's buttie.

'Same way as everybody else,' Arthur said innocently.

'Go on then, surprise me.'

'Tie a bit of string round the tail and drop it down your trouser leg,' Arthur said, pretending to be surprised that Brown didn't know. He took a long sip of his tea.

At his table, Herbert burst out laughing.

'Very clever,' Brown nodded. 'And you got it off the docks like that?'

'I'm here, aren't I?'

'You're a bloody liar, Arthur Cousins.'

'It's straight. Nobody noticed a thing. Not till I got on the tram, anyroad. That Sandra Greenwood. You know her, Harry. From Thrunscoe.'

'I remember her.'

'She gets on at Riby Square. She works at Johnson's Chemists. Comes and sits right next to me at the back of the tram. She allus fancied me. After a minute, she starts looking uncomfortable. "What's that, Arthur Cousins?" she says. I don't know how she noticed. "How'd you mean?" I ask her. "You know very well," she says, going bright red. "It's nothing," I says. I thought she was going to call the conductor. "Well, if it's nothing, it's leaking," she says, and gets off the tram. Corporation Street. That's two miles from where she lives. I could have lost five bob if she'd kept going on.'

'Boats are in,' Herbert shouted as they all laughed at Arthur and Brown stood behind his counter frowning furiously. 'He'll catch you every time, Peter,' Herbert laughed, finishing his tea and banging the cup down on the counter. 'You not knowing local ways, like.'

'Go to buggery, Herbert.'

'No, it's right. I'm only trying to be helpful.'

'I don't know why I let you in this café, Arthur,' Brown

4

grumbled as Harry and Herbert pulled their duffel coats on and opened the café door. 'Did you want this bacon buttie?'

'Course. I'm not going out there. It's bloody freezing. And rough.'

Herbert was already half-way across the promenade when Harry followed him. The wind had lifted in the last hour, whipping off the sea and driving the waves against the pier, and at the estuary, the afternoon sky was black with rain and clouds. The lighthouse on Sanctuary Point blinked on and off steadily, and a couple of trawlers were steaming up the river for the next market.

At the slipway, two boats were already in, and half a dozen Land Rovers waited for the rest. Harry went down to George's boat and stood at the edge of the breakwater, the icy water washing against his wellingtons, the wind cutting into his face.

George cut the engine and leap-frogged over the side of the boat into the freezing tide. It came almost to the top of his waterproofs. Steve, his brother, began to reverse the Land Rover down the slipway. As George waded up to Harry, he shouted directions to his brother and nodded to Harry.

'Bloody awful weather.'

'All right?'

'Nearly lost her over Binks Sands. Must be force nine.'

'Good trip?'

''Bout sixty stone, codling mostly. Grab hold of the bows, then.'

They manhandled the little boat up on to the slipway and waited for Steve to get the Land Rover into position. The slipway was greasy with oil and seaweed, and they had to hold on to the sides of the boat to keep their balance steady. Herbert was helping with the other boat. The sky was darkening rapidly, the promenade deserted and dark apart from Brown's café. The air was full of flying spray, and above the little boats, herring-gulls swarmed and squabbled, diving for the fish that lay in the open hold.

When the Land Rover was in position, Steve put the

handbrake on and jumped out to help hoist the boat up on to the frame. It took them fifteen minutes to guide the boat into place and get it lashed safely down, the waves tumbling in against their legs all the time, the wind freezing their hands and reddening their faces.

Up on the road, Arthur stood and watched them, huddled into his coat.

'That mate of yours is a big help,' George cursed when they'd got the boat into place. He wiped his face with the back of his hand, smearing oil across his forehead.

'Done my bit,' Arthur shouted back from the railings. 'Down the docks since six this morning.'

George snorted his derision.

'They'll sort you out, once you get to Catterick,' he scoffed.

Arthur was eighteen at the end of the year, the same as Harry, and like most of the lads from their streets would be going straight to Catterick unless he joined the trawlers. Signing up for the distant-water fishing granted exemption from national service, provided you stayed at sea until you were twenty-six. Harry had no intention of doing either.

'You going out tomorrow?' he asked George.

'Course I'm going out.'

'You'll want the bait then?'

'Got Margery's order to do next. She'll be complaining all weekend if I don't get her freezer filled before Friday.'

Like most of the inshore fishermen, George supplied several local fish and chip shops with fresh fish. What he couldn't sell that way, Steve took down to the seven o'clock market on the fish docks. Arthur sometimes helped him to sell it, muddling it in with the good stuff from the trawlers.

'You going for a drink?' George asked, rubbing his hands and slapping Harry on the back.

'No, thanks. About the worms . . . ?'

'Same as today.'

Taking his wallet from his jacket pocket, George counted out a week's money and stuffed the notes into Harry's hand.

'Good bait, Harry. You must know where to dig.'

'Been watching Herbert.'

'He's the man, right enough. Ready then, Steve?'

Another boat was heading for the slipway and Herbert's man had already driven off with his boat bouncing behind on the trailer. Herbert walked across, peering into the back of George's boat.

'Not much money in codling, George.'

'Enough for me.'

'Flatties, that's what you want to be after.'

'And where am I going to sell them, Herbert?'

'Prime fish. Lovely whites. Going for a drink?'

They walked off together up the slipway, shouting good-night above the wind. Out beyond the pier, two more boats were chugging towards the slipway, their engines racing against the tide, flashlights flickering and lifting on the water. As Steve drove off, another Land Rover took his place. He would be taking the fish straight to the shops they supplied. Harry watched the other boats being landed, and then walked up the slipway to Arthur.

Two

Arthur climbed over the railings and jumped down to the slipway as Harry reached the top. He slipped his arm through Harry's.

'Fish and chips,' he said firmly as they walked up the broad esplanade back into town. Ahead of them, a tram rattled along the dismally lit road, heading for the Winter Gardens, and the sign on the roof of the Regal flashed on and off.

'You're allus eating,' Harry said.

'I'm allus hungry. Keith said he might be there. He's got summat to tell us.'

'He's not got his papers?'

'I think so.'

'Christ.'

Arthur was short and broad-shouldered, with a flat, round face and black hair cropped close to the head. At fourteen he'd had some tattoos done on both arms, one of a mermaid and one of a skull. He told the social worker he'd done it to upset his mother. He was expelled from school for fighting and causing trouble. When he got into fights, he seemed to lose his mind, spitting and punching in a frenzy, his eyes a funny, colourless blank. He lived in the terraces behind the promenade, the rows of back-to-backs local people called fishermen's lanes. His father had been drowned in the North Sea when he was eight, and now that his brother Patrick had signed up as a deckhand, there was just Arthur and his mother. On the day Patrick went to sign up as an apprentice galley-boy, his mother clung to his arm, shrieking and wailing as he dragged her half-way along the street. In the struggle, she lost one of her shoes.

'You just keep away from him,' Harry's mother always

said when she knew they were hanging around together. She would never say why she didn't like the Cousinses. Harry had gone to Arthur's house once for some lugworms to use as bait. Arthur dug for the worms when he was still at school, working the foreshore at five and six o'clock in the morning.

'He don't need the money, love,' Arthur's mother grinned at Harry when he was standing awkwardly in their back yard. 'I gives him all the money he needs.'

She was leaning against the door. She had jet-black hair and her arms were covered with the sores she'd got from the filleting. She'd worked for years down the docks, filleting the cod and haddock, and the salt they used as a preservative had eaten into her skin.

'You heard about the herring-gulls?' Arthur asked, lighting a cigarette and offering the packet to Harry.

'No.'

'Somebody's been blowing 'em up again. Off the pier end.'

'I hadn't heard.'

'Didn't Herbert say owt?'

'No.'

Arthur shrugged and dragged at his cigarette.

'Fucking kids,' he said.

They both laughed.

'I shall have to get some stuff,' Arthur sighed. 'Show 'em how to do it properly.'

'Do us a favour.'

They turned left along the top road overlooking the ornamental gardens and the promenade. A thin drizzle of rain blew into their faces, cutting in the cold wind, and the dim streetlights shone on the wet road and on the tram tracks.

'You should see the blokes on the docks,' Arthur went on. 'They catch rats as big as your arm and do the same trick.'

'With calcium carbonate?'

'Big as your arm.'

Harry shuddered.

'That's disgusting.'

9

'Drop 'em in sacks and fling 'em in the harbour.'

'I don't know how you work down there, Arthur.'

'Better than the dole.'

'There's other jobs.'

'Or the army.'

They were both silent. Down on the promenade, they saw the lights in Brown's café go out. That meant all the inshore fishing boats were safely landed. The pier and promenade were completely deserted, black in the winter cold. At the estuary, the foghorn on the lightship started to clang its dismal warning. Beyond the estuary, the lights of several trawlers rode the green swell.

'You're not thinking about George Bainbridge?' Arthur said when Harry remained silent. 'You should take no fucking notice.'

'No.'

'What's he fucking know, anyroad?'

There was a queue already waiting outside Ted & Blue's.

Harry pushed his hands deeper into his pockets. He was thinking about the army. The lads coming back from Catterick, looking as though their heads had been boiled.

He shivered.

'You remember Ronald Timms,' he said. 'The night he showed us how to make calcium pellets.'

'That bastard.'

'He's in the army now.'

'Best place for him.'

'Must nearly have done his two years.'

In the queue outside Ted & Blue's, they could see Keith, standing with his shoulders hunched against the rain and wind.

'Come on,' Arthur said impatiently. 'I'm dying of starvation. Let's go and get summat to eat.'

'You lot look happy,' Ted beamed over the counter when they got inside the fish shop. 'Jack's not won the pools has he, Harry?'

'Fat chance.'

Half a dozen women were collecting the evening supper, and Blue was frying a fresh batch of cod ready for the next rush, the sweat pouring down his face, his arms pitted with white scars from the fat. They were brothers who had worked together on the distant-water trawlers, and saved enough money to buy the chippy. As Blue sweated over the deep fryers, Ted kept up a stream of chat with the people in the queue.

'How's your mother keeping, Harry?' he shouted as he wrapped up a double order of fish, chips and mushy peas. 'Still working at the Rialto, is she?'

'Regal,' Harry told him.

'That's the one. What they showing there then?'

'Rubbish usually,' one of the women guffawed.

'*Enticement*,' Arthur shouted before Harry could answer. Everybody in the queue laughed. ' "She was a tigress," Arthur recited, "exciting, dangerous and untamed." '

'Sounds like my old man,' another woman giggled.

Ted winked at his brother, nodding towards Arthur.

'It's the man from Laramie, Blue,' he grinned.

'I like Victor Mature meself,' one of the women interrupted. 'He's got wonderful eyes.'

'And Tony Curtis,' another woman sighed.

'Chips, mushy peas and scraps three times please,' Keith gave the order when they reached the till.

'Big spenders.'

'We're celebrating,' Arthur announced.

'*You've* won the pools?'

'Keith's failed his medical.'

'No I haven't.' Keith blushed.

'You said you had.'

'That's nowt to celebrate,' the woman immediately behind them said. 'My son failed his and we'd have been glad to be shot of the bugger.'

'Plenty of scraps, Ted,' Harry said, leaning across the counter and watching Ted heap the chips into the newspaper.

'You always get plenty at Ted & Blue's. What's wrong with you then, lad? Got flat feet?'

'I haven't failed,' Keith said angrily.

'I thought you said you had,' Arthur apologised.

Keith thumped him hard in the ribs and several of the women were laughing, watching what was going on.

'What's the matter with you, love?' the woman nearest Keith asked. 'You look all right. Is it your feet?'

'There's nowt wrong with his feet,' another woman giggled.

Keith was going bright red.

'I'm bloody fed up with you lot,' he said angrily, spilling vinegar on the counter and floor.

'Sorry, I'm sure.'

'No need to lose your temper, lad.'

'I got my papers,' Keith said furiously, his eyes suddenly shining with tears. 'I got my papers.'

He slammed the vinegar bottle down on the counter and walked out.

After paying, Harry and Arthur followed him.

'I was going to work for my dad,' Keith said as they sat in one of the shelters on the promenade.

They could hear the sea pounding against the seawall, a high wind throwing waves right over the railings, surf thundering into the metal struts of the pier.

'I was going to learn the business,' Keith went on. 'You have to know what you're doing, making prescriptions. It's a very responsible job.'

Keith lived with his parents in the flat above the chemists in the High Street. He was tall and nervous. He liked the musicals on the pier and went with his parents every Saturday night during the summer. He'd seen Alma Cogan and Teresa Brewer one summer, and kept talking about their sequinned dresses and the men in red tuxedos who took the tickets on the doors and helped with the grand piano.

'You can do it when you come back,' Arthur said.

'I was going to do it now.'

Harry finished the last of his food, saving a mouthful of mushy peas and scraps for last. He sucked his fingers clean and relaxed back against the wooden seat. It was damp with the cold and driving rain.

'I sometimes come here with Alison,' he said.

'Dirty bugger.'

'She's all right, Alison,' Keith said.

Standing up, Harry leaned in the doorway of the shelter and felt the rain wet on his face. He felt tired. He lit a cigarette and thought about Alison. She was doing her exams for university this summer. He was supposed to be seeing her next week, when Town had another home fixture. If she wasn't busy studying, they could go to the cinema afterwards.

'Let's go and get a drink,' Arthur said.

Harry straightened up and nodded.

'At the Dolphin,' he agreed.

Keith didn't move.

He hadn't eaten his food.

'You coming, Keith?'

'Where?'

'We'll go to the Sunnyside,' Arthur said. 'Buy you a pint.'

'All right.'

He got up and dropped the chips and peas into one of the rubbish bins just outside.

As they walked along the promenade back into town, the rain drove into their faces, and Arthur started singing, trying to shout above the noise of the wind. Harry joined in, linking his arm with Keith's. They sang Rosemary Clooney's 'Hey There', their voices lost in the gusts of wind, the steady crash of waves pounding against the promenade.

Three

The Sunnyside Club was down Orwell Street, behind the main fish docks. The club was just a large room on the top floor of a disused warehouse. On the second floor was a snooker hall, and a chandler rented the ground floor for his shop, selling waterproof clothes and fishing gear for the ships. As they walked from the tram, they could smell the fish offal on the market, the stink blown on the wind that lashed through telegraph wires and whistled between the deserted buildings. It was an area serving the fish docks – small businesses and early morning cafés, and by late afternoon the only places open were the clubs and the Fishermen's Home.

'We should have gone to the Dolphin,' Harry grumbled as they reached the stairs up to the club. 'It's a bloody graveyard, this dump.'

'You'll be all right then,' Arthur grinned.

The darkened street was empty. Later, taxis would be parked outside the club, waiting. When the fishermen got off the trawlers, the younger ones hired taxis for the three day turnaround and they went from club to club, drinking and picking up lasses. The girls went down on the lockpit whenever a ship was due in for the market.

When they got upstairs, the place was empty except for the owner and a girl busy cleaning the tables.

'Not you fucking lot,' Tony sighed when they pushed through the doors and clattered into the dimly lit room. 'Thought I was going to get some trade.'

'Three pints please,' Arthur shouted across the room, pulling his coat off and throwing it over the back of a chair. 'Keith's skipper.'

'That a fact?'

'No it's not,' Keith scowled.

'This is Elaine,' Tony said, getting the beers. 'Helping me out a bit. You want brown-ale, I'm assuming.'

'Only the best,' Harry said, sitting down and glancing at the girl.

She went on working. She looked about sixteen, plump and with dark curly hair, her nose very small and her mouth slightly open as she scrubbed at the tables. After each push of the cloth, she had to brush her hair out of her eyes.

They sat at one of the tables near the window. In the street, a dustbin lid clattered along the pavement. A thin shiver of cold air blew through the thick curtains. Taking his coat off, Harry shivered and rubbed his hands together. The walls of the club were covered with a thick plush wallpaper, garish red and shining when all the lights were turned on. Tony had most of the lamps turned off to save money. There were a dozen tables without tablecloths, enormous pink ashtrays in the shape of a woman's breast on each table. The ashtrays were Tony's particular pride. You rested your cigarette where the nipple stood out at the top of the ashtray.

'The thing about the Sunnyside,' Arthur said happily, 'is you don't get diverted by peanuts and bags of crisps.'

'And the beer's twice as expensive,' Keith muttered.

'Miserable sod.'

'Where's the girls, Tony?' Harry asked when Tony brought their drinks.

'Be at Yeung's this time of evening.'

Most of the prostitutes who worked the docks started the evening with a Chinese meal. Harry glanced at his watch. In the dismal room, he had forgotten the time. It was still only early evening, just after six o'clock. It felt like the middle of the night.

'You want the cards?' Tony asked, setting their drinks down on the table and wiping it quickly with a cloth.

'Thanks.'

'I've got some barrels to shift,' he told them. 'You want owt, you ask Elaine.'

While Arthur and Keith played cards, Harry sat and watched the girl. She was wearing a blue dress underneath her apron, and when she moved he could see her nipples against the soft material. She blushed slightly as she worked, knowing he was watching her. When she stopped to take a breath, she looked straight up at him, her eyes an intense, clear blue. He felt embarrassed. She stared at him, unconcerned, not saying anything, and he pretended to be watching the game. Arthur shouted at every bet, slapping the table and accusing Keith of cheating. They were playing brag, sixpence a hand. As Tony crashed about behind the bar, the girl went on with her scrubbing, and when she'd finished, brought the bucket round to the front of the bar where Harry could watch her and squeezed the cloth dry between both hands, twisting it for the last drop of water.

'You going to get us another beer, pet?' Arthur said when he saw she'd finished with the tables.

'If you like.'

'Three pints then. Sup up, Harry.'

She brought the drinks to their table, spilling some as she carried the tray.

'You can pay Tony,' she said, wiping her forehead with her bare arm. 'He doesn't like me to take the money.'

'Thanks,' Harry smiled.

'You haven't got a cigarette, have you?' she said.

'Yes, course.'

He lit the cigarette for her, offering the packet to Arthur and Keith. They went on with their game.

When the cigarette was lit, she took a long drag.

'Thanks.'

She had a nice voice, warm and cheerful. She spoke with a soft accent, not the hard edge of the coast.

'You work down the docks?' she asked.

'Arthur does. I do bait digging.'

'What's that?'

'Worms,' Arthur grinned at her. 'Twelve inches long, some of 'em.'

'That's horrible.' She shivered.

'You don't notice,' Harry told her.

'I couldn't do that.'

'You get used to it.'

'I don't like this place either,' she said, looking round the empty club. 'It's a dump. I'm not stopping here.'

'You want to go down the curing houses,' Arthur said. 'Plenty of work there.'

'I'm going down the fairgrounds this summer,' she said, ignoring Arthur. 'You can gets jobs down there easily, can't you?'

'Yes,' Harry laughed. 'That's where I work, in the season.'

'Oh?'

'At Happiland.'

'Is that a fairground?'

'Next to Wonderland.'

'I've never been down there,' she said. 'My dad's on a farm. Out at Bicker. That's miles from here. I'm staying with my aunt. It's horrible. I want a job where I can live in.'

She took a deep drag at her cigarette and opened her mouth, letting the smoke rings drift lazily up to the filthy ceiling. Harry watched them slowly disintegrate, and then looked back at the girl. She smiled, watching him absent-mindedly.

'I could show you round Happiland,' Harry suggested.

'When?'

'On Sunday?'

'Won't it be shut?'

'Somebody might be down there.'

She smiled vaguely.

'You think there's going to be a flood?' she asked, not taking her eyes off his face.

'Bad weather coming.'

'I'd like it to flood.'

Outside in the street, they could hear taxi doors slamming. A woman shrieked with laughter.

'Mac might have some work.'

17

'Who's he?'

'He owns Happiland.'

'That would be nice.'

'This Sunday then?'

'If you like.'

She finished her cigarette as two of the fishermen came into the club, slamming the doors back and yelling for Tony.

'It's fucking Arthur Cousins,' one of the fishermen shouted, colliding with the table near the door and hanging on to his friend's arm. 'Allus bloody boozing.'

Tony came through from the storeroom and glanced quickly at Elaine, rolling his sleeves up.

Going behind the counter, she told him they owed for three pints.

'You all right then, lads?' one of the fishermen grinned, lurching across to their table and sitting down with a thump of his head against the thick flock wallpaper.

Out on the stairs, there was scuffling and laughter, and the door slammed back again, two or three more men stumbling into the room, followed by some girls Harry didn't recognise.

'You've had a skinful, Martin,' Arthur said, shuffling the cards.

'I have, my beauty.'

Over by the door, Dave Pettitt slid slowly from his chair and sat with his back to the wall. One of the girls knelt down beside him and ruffled his hair, whispering something to him while the others found a table.

'That's Dorothy,' the fisherman sitting next to Harry nodded. 'You know she's got three kids? Wonderful lass. Get us a drink, Tony. Fill the glasses.'

Tony stood behind the bar. He had tattoos of anchors and women's names up both arms. The fishermen liked him because he'd spent years on the trawlers himself, working off Iceland and as far north as Greenland.

'Double whiskies all round?' Tony asked, already filling the glasses.

Two of the fishermen were dancing slowly in the middle of the room, clinging tightly to the women.

By the door, the woman called Dorothy was sitting with Dave Pettitt, listening to him snore and staring vacantly at the couples dancing. She had a tight green skirt on and it pulled right up her thighs when she sat down. The bottom of a tattoo showed beneath the edge of the skirt.

'You still digging bait, Harry?' Martin hiccuped, leaning close to Harry and squeezing his arm. His breath stank of whisky and cigarette smoke. He had a dead tab behind his ear and a cigarette in his hand.

'That's right.'

'It's no way of life, man.'

'I do all right.'

'No way of life.'

Elaine brought a whisky to their table and held it out for Martin. His hand wobbled as he took the drink, trying not to spill any.

'You could have put it down, lass.'

'Sorry.'

'You wanta go for a drink?'

'No thanks.'

'Bit of a dance?'

Lurching to his feet, Martin held the table with one hand and began to dance by himself in front of the bar. The other couples watched him, the women shrieking with laughter, the men grinning and smoking, their eyes bleary with drink. Moving out of the way, Elaine got back behind the bar and told Tony he could take the drinks round himself. Martin went on dancing.

'This is the life,' Arthur said, shuffling the cards again and slapping them down in front of Keith. 'Another hand, Keith?'

'We ought to leave,' Keith said, glancing round at the men.

At the bar, Martin collapsed against the counter and sank slowly to the floor.

'You can't leave, lads,' he mumbled, grazing his face against the rough wood. 'You haven't bought a round.'

Fiddling with the radio, Tony tuned in to some dance music and turned the volume as loud as he could. The radio was old, and in the big room, the orchestra thumped hollowly. The couples started dancing again. By the door, Dave Pettitt snored loudly, his mouth wide open.

As Harry got up to leave, another woman came up the stairs, banging into the door and peering round the room uncertainly.

'Hello, Renee,' one of the men called, and waved.

She grinned at him vaguely.

'I thought you buggers was 'ere. Leaving us in the fucking bog.'

'That you, Renee?' Martin shouted.

'It is, my darling.'

'Come and give us a cuddle.'

Arthur finished his beer and shouted goodnight to Tony.

Behind the bar, Elaine was trying to tune the radio to Luxemburg.

She smiled and waved as Harry closed the door.

Out in the street, they could hear 'Rock Island Line'.

Four

It was gone ten o'clock when Harry got home. His boots echoed up the narrow passage between the houses, and as he unfastened the yard gate a cat leapt off the wall, crashing into the dustbins and screeching as Harry kicked out. He could hear the television booming next door in Mrs Blakey's, and across the backs, a man and woman were standing at a curtained window, kissing. Fastening the gate, Harry watched them. He leant against the top of the gate, feeling the damp wood against his face. At the racket of the dustbins the couple separated and stood facing each other, not moving. He wondered what they were saying. They were in the small back bedroom. It was Wilfred Lenton's house, and he knew Wilfred was away, fishing for mackerel off the Scottish coast. Mavis was a small, hot-faced woman, with tightly curled hair and breasts that pushed against anything she wore, as if her clothes were all too small for her. Whenever he met her in the street he felt like crossing the road, embarrassed by her warm smiles.

When the bedroom light went out, he let himself into the kitchen and hung his coat on the back of the door. His mother wouldn't be back from the cinema for another half hour, and his grandfather was crouched at the table, puzzling over the football pools. When Harry turned the tap on to fill the kettle, Jack looked up and stared at him absent-mindedly, deep in thought.

'You think Town are going to win this week, Harry?'

'Against Millwall! I should hope so.'

'They're going to need DeGruchy.'

'They've got him, haven't they?'

His grandfather sniffed. In the quiet, the fire leapt suddenly in the grate, and the wind moaned down the passage between the houses.

'You know they were in the First Division when I was working the White Sea?' his grandfather said.

'You want some tea?'

'Finest team you've ever seen.'

On the mantelpiece, a coronation coach and horses stood between the clock and an egg-timer Harry's mother had won on the fairgrounds. It was a model of a lighthouse, with a flat top so that you could turn it over when the sand had run through. There were photographs of Harry's mother and father on the sands, and one of his grandparents, taken before his grandmother died in 1926. His grandmother had had long red hair, right down to the bottom of her back. She was bigger than Jack, a heavy, round-faced woman with determined eyes. The first time Jack had come home drunk, she'd taken a picture off the wall and brought it straight down over his head, leaving the frame stuck round his shoulders so that a neighbour had to come and saw him free. It was a story Jack liked to tell himself.

Harry made the tea and sat down at the table with his grandfather. They let the tea brew and then Harry poured two strong mugs. In the grate, the fire burned low, and the range felt warm. Some washing was strung across the front of the range, airing.

'Did you really brew tea in an urn?' Harry asked, sipping at his own mug. 'Herbert Edlin was saying how you used to chuck packets of tea and sugar in together and boil it for weeks.'

'Needed it strong.'

As he spoke, Jack drank his tea with his good hand. His left hand had been amputated at the wrist. On his last trip, steaming for cod off Iceland, he'd gone up to the whaleback to help hack the ice from the rigging, and forgotten to keep his gloves on. When a big wave took the ship starboard, he lost his footing on the metal steps and fell to the deck, cutting his head open and reaching out for the railings for support.

By the time he realised what was happening, his fingers were frozen to the metal. They had to cut his hand off with him lying there, screaming and raving as they poured rum down his throat. Now, he had an artificial hand. He tapped with it nervously on the table, concentrating on the football coupons.

Harry put another spoon of sugar into his tea and yawned.

In the yard, the gate banged furiously against the hinges, and the carpet in the front room lifted off the floor as a gust of wind howled through the house.

'That's a wind,' Jack said quietly, looking up. ''Bout force ten I reckon.'

Harry glanced at the clock, wondering how long his mother would be.

'Gaffers used to put nails in the tea, you know,' his grandfather said abruptly, staring at the football coupons.

'You what?'

'Give a false weight, you see. Days of the smacks, that was. The crew used to pay part of the cost of the trip. Fuel and tackle and some of the grub. Gaffers used to put nails at the bottom of the sacks of tea. You wouldn't know till you'd got down to the bottom. And they charged. They owned all the suppliers, you see. Coal, salt, ice. Owned everything. Cunning buggers.'

'Crooked, you mean.'

'They didn't get it all their own road.'

His grandfather had short white hair and the thick arms of a fisherman. His hand was scarred with small cuts from the gutting. He'd never gone in for tattoos. Said they were for gypsies. When he got into arguments his face went nearly purple, his eyes shining very blue against his tanned skin. His face and arms were tanned nearly mahogany. He had a long cut up the side of his face where a winch wire had snapped and gone flying through the air, flicking the side of Jack's face and cutting another man's leg off.

'You shouldn't drink you know, Harry.'

'She won't know.'

'You stink like a brewery, lad.'

'Tea'll cover it.'

They heard the footsteps coming up the passage, and Harry got up to freshen the teapot. His mother worked all day in the laundry up the road, and at nights she had a job as usherette in the Regal. There were a dozen cinemas in the town. She had to help clean the place up after the last film, and usually came home exhausted.

'Is that tea fresh?' She smiled tiredly as Harry opened the kitchen door for her, the freezing wind gusting through the kitchen as he got the door shut once she was inside. He helped her off with her coat and scarf and went to hang them behind the stairs door. Sitting down at the table, she took the mug of tea Jack poured for her and glanced at the pools. As she moved the paper, Harry noticed that her arm was stained with the yellow ointment they used at the laundry when one of the women got burnt on the scalding steam-presses.

'You're not putting Town for a draw, Dad,' she said with surprise, smiling at him and pushing the coupon back. 'That's not like you.'

'Don't do me no favours, do they?' he snorted.

'They're on a winning streak, Jack,' Harry pointed out.

'Who's filling this thing in?'

Harry sat down again at the table and yawned. He felt tired, but didn't want to go to bed. The kitchen was his favourite room, especially on winter nights like this. He liked just sitting by the range, listening to the wind beat against the windows, his mother reading or sewing, listening to the wireless. When he was ill as a child, she would let him lie on the sofa by the fire while she got on with her jobs, and he was quite content, hearing her coming and going. On summer nights it was different. They could sit on the doorstep then and shell peas into the colander, or just talk while she did some mending, the wireless humming in the background. But that wasn't like the winter. He closed his eyes now and listened to the two of them talking. His mother was complaining about the film, some insipid comedy starring Fred Emney and Cardew Robinson. She wondered why people paid good money to watch such rubbish.

'Not that they watch much of it,' she muttered, finishing her tea and leaving a ring of lipstick round the cup. 'You should see the state of that cinema. I don't think we should have to clean up after people like that. They should get cleaners. He's dead mean, that Mr Mortimer. I'd give it up if I could afford it, go back to the bakery.'

Harry opened his eyes and frowned.

'No you wouldn't, Mother,' he said.

When she worked at the bakery, she used to start at four in the morning and finish at seven, so that she could see him off to school before going to the laundry for nine o'clock.

'You'll not go there again,' Harry said. 'We're not that badly off.'

'I know, love. It's not the money.'

'Give it up then.'

'It's just the stupid films we have to watch. And a few people, you know, the way they behave.'

At the table, Jack grunted and shifted in his seat.

'You know what I think,' he said, getting up and glaring at Harry.

'Shut up, Dad.'

'If he had a proper job . . .'

'Go to bed.'

'I am, don't worry. Just speaking my mind.'

Taking the papers with him, Harry's grandfather sniffed again and left the kitchen, stumping up the stairs and slamming the bathroom door. When he'd gone, Harry's mother laughed and reached out, touching his hand. He yawned and stretched. He had been up since before dawn.

He watched his mother as she finished her tea. She had hair that had been as red as his grandmother's, but it was cut short now and was losing its flame colour. And her eyes were green. He thought about Arthur and the fish shining green from the floor of the ocean. His grandfather hadn't got green eyes, they were deep blue, fading now to white. He wondered whether his grandmother had had green eyes, and somehow knew she had. But he was too tired to ask. He heard the clock striking eleven-thirty, and got up from the table to wash the tea things.

'Leave those, love,' his mother said. 'You look dead on your feet. What time are you working?'

'Not early.'

'Aren't you digging?'

'I've got enough frozen for George. I'll get some fresh later in the week.'

Kissing his mother goodnight, he went up to the small bedroom at the back of the house that had been his ever since he was a child. He undressed in the bathroom, left his clothes ready for morning, and got into the narrow single bed in the darkness. He liked to sleep with the curtains drawn back and the window open. Whatever the weather, he always left his window open. He liked the cold, the sound of the rain and the wind, the foghorns out on the estuary. Now, when he lifted the window off the latch, the wind blew the curtains into his face and rattled his bedroom door. Getting into bed, he pulled the sheets up around his neck and listened to the gale, the distant roar of the sea, the telegraph wires lashing in the storm.

When his father was alive, he used to throw the sheet and blankets back sometimes and pretend he was on a trawler's bridge, keeping watch in the deckhouse in the Arctic night, watching the huge seas swell and tumble beneath the ship as the herring-gulls followed the ship's wake, screaming and mourning above the whaleback. In freezing cold weather, he would lie naked in his bed, listening to the foghorns, the low wash of the surf in Suggitt's Bay, the warning bell at the estuary clanging through the winter cold. When he was completely frozen, shivering with cold, he would pull the bedding back and curl up into the warmth, imagining he was in his bunk on a trawler, warm and tired while the shift on deck went on with the relentless gutting and mending of the trawl, hacking at the frozen fish with razor-sharp knives, swaying with every movement of the ship as the engines kept up their thumping, comforting rhythm.

He went to sleep with the sound of the gale, howling down the narrow streets, the sea booming against the seawall and the rusting struts of the pier. He closed his eyes, and thought about Elaine, staring at him with her warm, indifferent smile.

Five

In the morning, Harry unpacked some frozen bait from the fridge he kept in the yard shed and delivered it to George Bainbridge.

'I'm not going out,' George told him, eating his breakfast and listening to the short-wave radio. 'You hear this lot?'

On the wireless, skippers were talking cheerfully about the weather, their voices crackling with static as they argued about plots and currents, the best way to get out of the river. The quickest course was to turn sharp north from the estuary and risk Binks Sands, but in this weather going so close to Sanctuary Point could be disastrous.

George's wife put the worms in their own freezer and poured Harry some tea.

'I'm glad he's listening to me for once,' she told Harry. 'We're not so badly off he should drown.'

George shushed her so that he could hear the radio, straining forward so as not to miss a word. Like all fishermen, he could never get enough of the sea. Even at home he had to be in touch with what was happening, on the river or out beyond the six mile wide estuary.

Harry drank his tea and walked round to Arthur's. There was no market on a Saturday and Arthur always had a lie in.

'Is he up?' Harry said when Arthur's mother opened the kitchen door. She looked as if she'd got straight out of bed herself, scowling into the daylight and rubbing her eyes. Her make-up had smudged overnight, and she'd obviously gone to bed with her ear-rings on, a red weal angry on her cheek.

In Arthur's bedroom, Harry sat on the bed while Arthur got dressed. There was a large chart of the river on Arthur's wall. He was obsessed with the river, the banks and dangerous tides, Sunk Island and Trinity Sands, Spurn Bight and Hedon Haven.

'Force ten, according to the wireless,' Harry told him as Arthur struggled into a thick jumper and fastened his boots. 'You fancy the reserves?'

'I fancy that lass.'

'What lass?'

'The one you didn't notice at the Sunnyside.'

'We could go and see *The Last Frontier*,' Harry grinned. 'Or the boxing. They're opening the pier specially for the lightweight regionals.'

'Fuck off, Harry. You ready?'

'I am.'

'Let's go and see what the sea's doing.'

When they got down to the promenade, the tide was right out, a line of surf raging at the horizon. They ran down the cut beside the Regal, the gale buffeting them violently against walls and railings and the rain lashing into their faces. Out on the promenade, it was difficult to stand up. Bits of paper and wrack from the foreshore blew along the open road. It was freezing cold, and the promenade was deserted.

'Let's go to Brown's,' Arthur shouted above the wind, the hood of his coat flapping round his face. 'All right?'

They ran down the arcade of amusement centres and cafés and forced the door open into Brown's café. It was packed. The windows were steaming up with heat and tobacco.

'Not you again,' Brown grinned when Arthur got to the counter.

'Can't keep away, Peter,' Harry explained. 'It's your bacon butties.'

'And I'm the only place open.'

They got bacon butties and tea and sat down at one of the window tables, wiping the condensation with their elbows so that they could see out to the promenade and the foreshore.

'This is going to be great,' Arthur said, spooning sugar into his tea and getting his cigarettes out of his coat pocket. 'There's nowt better than a really good storm.'

'And a cup of tea,' Harry nodded.

All afternoon, the wind gathered force.

Brown's was crowded with fishermen and bait diggers come to watch the sea breaking over the seawall. The windows constantly steamed up and the air stank of strong shag tobacco. On the counter, a wireless gave out sports reports, and the juke box played Alma Cogan and Dickie Valentine, Ruby Murray and David Whitfield. Several of the fishermen knew Harry and Arthur, and joked about it being safer out at sea, steaming after cod off North Cape or round the frozen wastes of Cape Kanin and Novaya Zemlya.

Late in the afternoon, Herbert Edlin came and sat at their table and told them an endless yarn about lugworms. According to Herbert, the female only got the urge to procreate just before the big tides of a full December moon. She carried the spawn inside her in a bag which kept growing until it burst her skin and killed her. The male then scattered his sperm on top and the movement of the tides washed them together and fertilised them. In fifty years of digging, Herbert had never heard the word hermaphrodite, and when one of the fishermen tried to explain, Herbert looked at him as if he were half behind the door.

As darkness fell, the wind began to veer to the north.

The noise in the café was deafening. Static distorted the wireless. Waves twenty feet high lashed the pier and promenade, thudding into the reinforced concrete seawall. In the heat and excitement, men shouted above the din of the juke box, making bets about the height of the tide, arguing about the strength of the sea defences. They could hear the iron struts of the pier screaming and vibrating under the weight of water, and high above the clouds of spray, herring-gulls wheeling and mourning, battling to fly inland away from the storm.

At five o'clock, Brown decided it was time to close, and asked some of the men to help him hammer the wooden shutters into place. The metal bars were rusty with lack of use. Water flooded round the men's feet in black, icy eddies, and some of them began to panic, saying there was no use putting shutters up if the sea was going to come over the wall. They began arguing, and Brown started to shout abuse, hammering at the shutters with a wedge. As the final bar was fixed, an enormous wave hit the café on the pier, and smashed the windows, the gale suddenly rising to a shriek, howling up the passages between the small cafés and ramshackle amusement arcades.

Harry and Arthur turned and ran towards the railway station. They scrambled up the concrete steps, slipping as the sea surged across the promenade behind them, grazing their hands on the rough concrete. The wind tugged and lashed at their coats. As they ran up the narrow cut beside the station, they could hear the huge green swells, thundering into the promenade, thumping and vibrating the ground. An ambulance wailed along the cliff road. Harry suddenly felt frightened, thinking about the low railway embankment that separated fishermen's lanes from the sea. They were both soaked to the skin, their teeth chattering uncontrollably as they ran home through the blistering wind.

The tide came over the seawall at seven o'clock, just after Harry's mother had lit a fire in the front bedroom and made a flask of tea. She put candles on the dressing table and window sill, and a dry box of matches. Minutes later, the lights fused.

'Better be getting upstairs,' Harry's grandfather said, and began to lock the back door and pile rugs at the doorjamb. The wireless crackled, and Harry's mother turned it off, pulling the plug from the wall. In the range, the fire guttered and glowed angrily, flames leaping up the chimney as the wind rattled the doors and windows, and lifted the carpet off the floor in the front room.

They were sitting in the bedroom when the sea came down the narrow streets. There was a crashing sound as the tide broke over the railway embankment and ripped the wooden fencing out of the ground, and then a long silence as the water surged between the houses and the wind, for several seconds, dropped, veering to the south before turning back against the houses. Across the street, the neon lights flickered, and went out. Harry stood with his grandfather at the bedroom window, trying to see through the pouring rain.

The kitchen door splintered with a sharp crack, and then the windows in the front room shattered, the wind suddenly shrieking through the house and the letterbox banging frantically as if somebody was trying to break the door down. They heard the water hit the door between the front room and the kitchen, and then the furniture knocking against the walls, washed backwards and forwards by the waves. Harry's mother screamed, holding her hand to her mouth, her eyes white in the darkened bedroom.

'It's all right, pet, it's all right,' Jack muttered, holding Harry's mother in his arms.

In the house opposite, Mrs Lewis stood at an open window and yelled abuse at her husband who was struggling to pile sandbags at his front door. Her voice rose and fell with the wind, 'Bastard, stupid bastard,' carried away on the sudden squalls, flinging back when the wind changed direction. As they watched, they saw a man knocked over by the waves, clinging to a lamppost, desperately trying to get to his house. Several people had lit bedroom fires. In the chimney, the wind howled and whined, and the rain lashed at the windows. 'Bastard,' cried the voice in the wind, 'stupid fucking bastard.'

Six

The quiet and the smell were the first things they noticed in the morning.

Stagnant water lapped between the houses. The pumping station had broken down and the sewers were emptying into the streets. Dead rats and turds floated among the wreckage of crockery and saucepans. Ornaments and battered armchairs spun in slow circles over the broken drains. Above the debris, herring-gulls swarmed and squabbled, scavenging for food among the filth. As Harry helped his mother and grandfather lift the sodden carpet, two policemen waded down the street asking people if they needed any help, and a boy paddled up the road in a canoe, his oar draped with black seaweed.

Seawater a foot deep had flooded through the house. The walls were stained a dirty brown. Carpets were ruined. A stale, rotting smell hung in the air, drying into the cold walls. In the kitchen, the water had emptied the fire, carrying coal and ash everywhere.

Harry's mother began to cry as they struggled to move a settee.

'We'll never get this straight,' she said, sitting on the arm of a chair and weeping. 'It'll cost a fortune.'

'Don't you worry, pet.' Jack gasped for breath, patting her shoulder and sitting down next to her. 'Make us some tea, Harry.'

'Don't worry!' Harry heard his mother cry.

'I'll see to the furniture.'

'But it's ruined.'

'Then we'll buy new. I've got money, you know.'

'Oh, Dad.'

'Just give over fretting.'

Later in the morning, Harry went down to the promenade with Arthur.

He hoped he would be able to find Elaine, if she'd kept her promise.

'She won't come,' Arthur grinned, splashing up the street in his wellingtons.

'You never know.'

'I'm telling you. She's waiting for me.'

They climbed up on to the railway embankment and scrambled over the heaps of uprooted track. The sky hung over the town like a yellow bruise, and great banks of cloud were racing towards Sanctuary Point. At the estuary, four or five trawlers bobbed with the morning tide, waiting to go in for the Monday market. From the top of the embankment, they could see for miles, right along the foreshore. The sands and promenade were crowded with people. It was like midsummer, but cold in the icy wind.

The sea had littered the sands with debris, the retreating water carrying furniture and personal possessions from the houses, fruit machines and fairground equipment from the amusement centres, and dumping them on the beach. At the tideline, an armchair lurched drunkenly in the shallow water. A group of women shrieked and splashed up to their knees, trying to recover an empty pram. Waist-deep by one of the groynes, two men threw haphazard punches at each other over a sinking television set. Patiently, methodically, the beachcombers worked along the shores, combing the wreckage for anything of value, sifting through the sands for coins. There were hundreds of people out in the cold sunlight, scrabbling among cookers and ruined furniture, mattresses and children's toys, sodden clothes and battered tins of food. On the promenade, policemen stood outside the fairgrounds, protecting them from looters. A police car drove slowly up and down, flashing its blue light. On the site of what was left of the big wheel, a wooden horse stood alone on the sands, staring sightlessly out to sea.

The Arcadia, the second and smaller of the two piers, had

34

been demolished, and a tangled mass of girders and splintered wood lay on the sands. The electric light-bulbs that spelt Arcadia over the entrance had fragmented into a million coloured bits of glass, which shone and sparkled in the wintry sun. Fruit machines and lucky dips lay half-buried in the sand. Bagatelle tables stood upside-down among the piles of broken wood. Harry and Arthur spent half an hour searching through the ruins, and found dozens of fruit machine tokens, all of them marked Arcadia. They would never be able to use them.

'Fuck this,' Arthur said at last, stretching his back and staring round at the crowded sands. 'Let's go and get a drink.'

'Maybe we should see Mac,' Harry wondered.

'If he's here.'

Fed up, they climbed the steps to the promenade and walked along to Wonderland: The Biggest Covered Fairground In The World. Already, men were beginning the salvage operation. Bulldozers were shifting the sand. Lorries were loading up with equipment for repair. Engineers clambered up the big dipper, testing the wooden struts for damage and the tracks for metal fatigue. At the entrance, dozens of men were trying to lift the twisted shutters from their frame, so that a temporary door could be fitted.

In the smaller fairground next door, one of the stall owners was busy selling hot dogs and tea. Mac, the owner, was standing outside with Alison, staring up at the sign.

When Harry walked up, Alison smiled at him and took his arm.

Mac grimaced.

'You wouldn't think it was called Happiland,' he nodded to Harry. 'Bloody tides. This is all I need.'

At the far end of the fairground, somebody had lit a fire, and a juke box was playing Frankie Laine.

'You want any help, Mac?' Harry asked.

'No, I'm all right, I think. Bit of structural damage. Builders are going to have to sort that.'

'I could do a few days,' Harry said. 'Long as it doesn't interfere with the baiting.'

Mac shook his head and squeezed Harry's arm quickly.

'Thanks. You can come early for the maintenance. That's when I'll need help. Equipment's been knocked about a bit. We'll start the maintenance early. All right, Arthur?'

'Fine, thanks.'

Down by the juke box, two women in white aprons were dancing round the fire, and a crowd of men stood round and cheered. Everybody seemed determined that the fairgrounds would be ready for the new season, almost as though nothing had happened.

Harry told Mac he would come down next week and check, and they left Happiland and started walking back along the promenade. At his side, Alison clung to his arm, her hair blown across her face in the wind. From several of the amusements, music was now booming from the juke boxes.

'I didn't think you'd be down here,' Harry said as they walked along the top road towards the Winter Gardens.

'Why not?' Alison laughed.

'You're always studying,' Arthur chimed in, grinning at Alison. 'He's too thick to understand that.'

'I should think the whole town's down here,' Alison smiled, and reached up to kiss Harry quickly on the cheek. 'And I'm not always studying. We're going to the football next Saturday, aren't we?'

'So far,' Harry laughed.

They'd known each other since primary school, and had been going around regularly for years. When they first met, Dr Milburn had his house and surgery not far from the fishing community where most of his patients lived, but more recently, he had bought a bigger house at the other end of town. Harry and Alison grew up together, going to the cinema on Saturdays and attending the same school. Even his failing the eleven plus didn't make much difference, although Sheila Milburn told him he ought to find friends from his own school. Dr Milburn treated him just the same, absent-minded and vaguely friendly, and Harry took no notice. She was really Alison's stepmother, a tall, loud-voiced woman who spent her days briskly in the garden and her evenings playing bridge and complaining about her husband's patients. Harry saw Alison as often as he could, and put up with her stepmother's tight-lipped dislike.

They walked right down the promenade past the Winter Gardens and the boating lake and out along the stretch of coast called the Fitties. The road was covered with fine sand. The wind sang through the marram grass. Inland, the sea had flooded almost five miles, and the sun shone on water wherever they looked. Cows stood up to their bellies in fields of water. On one farm, chickens had settled on the roof for safety. They saw a pig, floating in the middle of a field on a settee.

'Is it bad, down your road?' Alison asked.

'Bloody mess.'

'It's still in the street,' Arthur explained. 'Pumping station broke down.'

'No.'

'The salt will be the problem,' Arthur said.

'Salt?'

'It gets into the walls. Shows through the paper. Doesn't matter how often you decorate.'

'How'd you know that?' Harry grinned.

'My mother's cousin. She had salt in the walls, years ago. Council keep treating it but it never shifts.'

Alison shook her head miserably.

'Can I do anything, Harry?' she asked.

Harry shrugged.

'We'll get new carpets. It's all right.'

'But your mother . . . ?'

'Jack's helping,' Harry said. 'He likes that.'

'It makes him feel needed,' Arthur said in a solemn voice.

'And gives him something to do.'

They walked right out to the huge lock at Tetney before

they saw the vehicles, a police car and army Land Rover parked down a lane about three miles out of town. Walking down the lane, they stopped and watched. Two policemen were wading out across the field towards a tree, carrying a short ladder. The soldiers leant on the gate, smoking and watching, messages from their jeep wireless crackling in the cold air, the voices of the policemen carrying over the field. A swarm of crows circled noisily up above, angry at being disturbed.

'You kids all right?' one of the soldiers asked.

His face was black with stubble, his eyes red and tired.

'We're fine,' Alison told him.

'Maybe you should go on,' the soldier suggested, but when they didn't move, he shrugged and turned back to watch what was happening in the field.

The policemen had reached the tree that stood in the middle of the field. It was surrounded by water. They stood for some seconds, staring up into the branches. One of them spoke, saying 'Fucking hell,' and the laughter drifted back across the field. When the police propped the ladder against the tree and tried to get the man down from the branches, he rolled forward very slowly, crouching as if in a forward roll, plunging into the icy water. Part of his dressing-gown tore off and flapped against the frozen bark. In the silence, a low wind moaned off the sea. The policemen stood and watched him as he floated face-down in the black water.

Seven

During the week, Harry did as much bait digging as he could, trying to get ahead with his work. He had his alarm clock set for four-thirty every morning, but he woke early as he always did when he was going digging on a dawn tide. By the Friday, he was almost finished. George Bainbridge owed him nearly ten pounds. On Saturday, he would be seeing Alison for the football.

The house was completely silent when he woke.

He jumped out of bed and pulled his clothes on quickly, shivering in the bitter cold. He wore thick serge trousers and a couple of jumpers over his shirt, and waterproof socks you could buy from the chandlers on the docks. He crept downstairs without stepping on the loose floorboards, and in the kitchen heaped fresh coal on to the range, waiting for the kettle to boil. There was still no carpet in the front room, but his grandfather had already bought new rugs for the kitchen and the floor was warm from the fire. Outside, the yard was brilliant with moonlight, frost shimmering on the ground and the roofs of the houses opposite. When the kettle boiled, he made a strong mug of tea, and drank it quickly, warming his wellingtons in front of the range. Pulling his duffel coat on, he let himself out of the back door, collecting his fork and plastic buckets from the coal shed and walking silently up the passage and down the road towards the foreshore.

On the sands, his wellingtons made a slapping sound as he walked out towards the tideline. The tide was drawing out rapidly now, and his heavy boots crushed the soft casts of lugworms. At the tideline, he could see a figure already working the firm sand, and guessed it would be Herbert. Opposite Wonderland, there was a petrified forest buried deep beneath the sand, and just beyond that some of the best lugworm beds. Herbert knew every kind of lugworm there was, and the variety of sand they did best in. Where you got black mud under the surface, the worms usually wouldn't keep well in the hot weather, and then he always dug in rougher, coarse sand. The worms needed a thicker skin to work through the coarse stuff, and would survive better until he got them home for freezing. Over the years, he had shown Harry how to avoid the soft sand, where the digs were always poor.

He got digging as soon as he reached the tideline. He dug a dam of sand across the ebbing tide, and then dug down steadily into the hard sand. As he moved on, the holes he had finished filled with water. You had to watch out for weeverfish, buried half into the sand, their poisonous sting so painful you could sometimes need hospital treatment. Hundreds of sand-eels worked just below the surface, burrowing for molluscs and worms. Razor shells and mermaid's purse floated in the pools of icy water. At the strandline, sandhoppers and hundreds of waders scavenged all day, cleaning the evil-smelling wrack.

Harry had first gone digging when he was ten. His father used to take him down the coast, digging for their own bait and then line-fishing from the edge of the surf. It was his father who had first shown him one of the worms, ten inches long and with revolting stunted legs. On one of his turnabouts between trips, they'd gone butt-pricking down at Tetney, the ancient method of getting flatties where you fastened a barb to a shaft of wood, waded out into the shallow water of the creeks, and thrust the stang into the water. Flatfish like to lie in shallow water, their pigmentation a camouflage in the muddy creeks, and you could get half a dozen without trying. All you had to watch, Harry's father joked, was that you didn't stick the barbed blade into your foot. Dabs and flounders were the commonest fish caught.

As Harry worked, the sky over the estuary began to lighten. Soon the waders would be swarming along the sands.

Godwits and curlews were the ones that took the most lugworms, their long beaks stabbing down into the sands, their hungry cries haunting in the dark silence. Oyster-catchers and plovers, redshanks and knots followed. The knots came in huge flocks every winter. Dunlin were the smallest waders of all. Further inshore, the turnstones dug for food under stones. At the tide edge, the tiny sanderling ran backwards and forwards in swarms.

Looking up, Harry saw the thin line of light over the horizon. A trawler was heading down the river, steaming for Iceland. High in the dark sky, a tern was beginning to call, its restless 'tirrick' echoing along the shores. That would be a sandwich tern. The little tern had an abrupt 'kik-kik' of a call, and the arctic tern a sort of 'keerree' or 'keeyah'. Once the herring-gulls and huge great black-backed gulls began their screaming noise, you wouldn't be able to hear anything else at all.

At gone six, Herbert lifted his shovel and walked across to where Harry was working. He had a steady, long stride. Watching him, you couldn't believe he was eighty, two years younger than Harry's grandfather. They had grown up together in the days of the sailing smacks, and never met without having a row, both of them too stubborn to admit that the other knew anything at all about the fishing. According to Harry's father, Herbert knew every inch of the foreshore for miles along the coast, but nobody knew more about the distant-water fishing than Jack Ellis.

'Doing all right then?' Herbert called as he dumped his buckets by Harry's trail of holes. 'You should be, morning like this.'

On the promenade, they saw the lights in Brown's café go on, and a milkfloat turned down from the top road towards the pier, its tiny lights flickering in the darkness. Breakfast at Brown's was the best part of the early morning digging, but Harry still had half a bucket to fill if he was going to meet George's order.

'Not be long,' he grunted, straining his back at the shovel. 'Go on, if you want to.'

'No, you're all right, lad,' Herbert grinned. 'I'll have a smoke.'

He lit his pipe, and stood staring out towards the estuary. As Harry worked, he could smell the sweet tobacco on the cold air. Frost was glimmering on the bucket he had filled. He felt the cold through his wellingtons and thick socks, his hands numb from picking up the worms. He was just glad there was no wind. In February, the winds off the sea could freeze your bones. The frost wasn't so bad if you kept moving.

'You hear about the mollies?' Herbert said, stuffing more tobacco into his pipe.

Harry shook his head, breathing heavily. He was sweating. He could feel the back of his shirt wet with sweat.

'Off the pier,' Herbert said. 'Blowing 'em up.'

'Last night?' Harry said, surprised.

'Before the floods.'

'Oh.'

'Too much to do since.'

'Yes. Must be kids,' Harry added.

'Aye. Nobody else would round here.'

Harry stopped, wiping his forehead with the back of his sleeve.

'You know how they are down the docks,' he said.

'Aye, I do.'

'You can get the stuff easy enough.'

'They'd not if they knew,' Herbert said angrily.

Harry went back to his digging.

He knew Herbert was upset about the gulls. Old fishermen believed that their friends returned as mollies. You could tell who it was from the way the bird behaved, some noisy and argumentative, some greedy and always scavenging for food. If the mollies stayed with you when you steamed up the river, that might mean you were going to have a good trip. If they met you as you came back, you hoped they weren't bringing bad news. When you killed a mollie, you might be hurting an old friend, and the bad luck could stay with you for ever.

'I ever tell you about Alec Reid?' Herbert said now, getting his pipe going again. 'Lived down your terraces.'

'No.'

'He worked the White Sea mostly. Youngest skipper I knew, just after the war. He was married to a lass called Sarah. Daughter of a schoolteacher. She must have been soft, that girl. Soft heart. They got married just before the war, and Alec went on the minesweepers, like most fishermen. He worked the Arctic Convoys, Murmansk, Northern Patrol. Quiet sort of bloke. Always cheerful. He used to tell her about the things that happened. Most men didn't. You can't tell women everything. He told her all about it. Sinkings, mates drowned. I think he thought he were just talking. Telling her what was going on.'

Herbert paused, taking a long pull on his pipe. Clouds of smoke drifted around his head.

'She knew about the mollies, of course. You couldn't not, living down the lanes. Managed right through the war. Then when he went back to fishing, she turned odd. They never had any children. Miscarriage or summat. She couldn't have any. She said she knew he wouldn't come back. He found her, after one trip, out on the north jetty. Middle of the night. She was throwing great lumps of cake for the birds. Shouting his name. They had to put her in hospital in the end. If these lumpers knew that, they wouldn't be so clever.'

When Harry had filled his second bucket, they walked back across the sands to the promenade and climbed the steps to Brown's. Inside, the café was already steaming up, and Brown had a couple of breakfasts on the grill. He greeted them with his big shout, enjoying the early morning quiet, the smell of hot food. He had spent all week clearing the café up after the floods, washing the sand out and getting the

43

plate glass replaced. No serious damage had been done, and he was happy to be back in business.

Herbert and Harry were the only people in the café. They sat at a window table and ate bacon and eggs, sausages, mushrooms, fried bread and beans. They had a large pot of tea between them, and lumps of hot bread smothered with butter. When the food was gone, Harry wiped his plate clean with a piece of bread, finished his tea, and offered Herbert a cigarette. They sat smoking together, watching the light broaden over the estuary, the sky turn a beautiful opal blue, the clouds of herring-gulls and waders swarming along the tideline where they had just been digging.

Harry thought he could never be happy anywhere else but here. He had lived in the terraces all his life, and didn't want to go anywhere else. He could imagine being like Herbert, working the coast for years to come, finding casual work in the summer when there was always plenty of money because of the trippers. It was a way of life Alison couldn't understand. She was always studying for exams, thinking about going away to university. She had no idea why he liked the town, loved the sea and the foreshores. She hated it, she said, when they got into arguments about what he was going to do. He'd given up trying to make her understand. With the bait he had just dug he would have plenty of money for a good time. As he sat with Herbert and smoked another cigarette, he thought about tomorrow's game, and the film they might go and see at the cinema. He could worry about the rest later.

Eight

On the Saturday morning, Harry helped George repair the lines and fit a new set of snoods, the short lines that carried the hooks and were attached to the main lines every twelve or eighteen inches. Jack had taken his mother to the shops to buy new furniture. They were going to pay cash for everything, before the shops sold out of stock. Hundreds of people were trying to get the money to replace their damaged possessions. After his lunch, he walked up to the Winter Gardens to wait for Alison. He never met her at home now. When she arrived, she looked flustered and tired. She let him kiss her on the cheek, and then waited impatiently for the tram, tapping her foot on the pavement. When Harry asked her what was the matter, she said her stepmother had been in a bad mood, grumbling about her wasting time at football matches.

'With me, you mean,' Harry grinned, and Alison said nothing.

Her dark hair, down to her shoulders, was tied back in a pony-tail which made her look younger than seventeen. She was wearing a warm coat and scarf, and her eyes looked almost black against her pale, drawn face. When Harry slipped his arm through hers, she pulled away irritably, and then said she was sorry, jumping on the tram platform ahead of him and making her way upstairs.

The tram had to travel the length of the promenade from the Winter Gardens through town to the football ground. As they trundled along, blue sparks raining down from the overhead cables, Harry looked out of the window and watched the crowds making their way along the streets for the match. Away from the Winter Gardens, the houses got smaller and the streets narrower, and hundreds of people poured out of the terraced rows to join the crowd heading for the ground. It always excited Harry. He squeezed Alison's hand again, and this time she didn't pull away, sitting close to him and resting her head on his shoulder. Half-way to the ground, he wondered if she would fall asleep. He had never seen her looking so tired.

At the ground, Alison cheered up.

'I hope they win,' she shouted, excited by the thronging crowd. One week when they'd gone, her coat had got caught in the turnstiles, and everybody made a joke about women going to football. She wore a team scarf for years, until her stepmother threw it on the fire, saying it was ridiculous and didn't go with her eyes. They filed through the narrow turnstiles, Harry paying for both tickets, and made their way up to the home stand, a great range of concrete terraces, open to the wind from the sea, and sudden squalls of rain or snow.

There must have been twenty thousand people there already. Town were only in the Third Division, but this year they looked like getting promotion. Bill Shankly had started to make a first-rate team before he left to take over at Workington, and Allenby Chilton had gone on with the good work. Now, it seemed as though nothing could stop them, and with Bill Evans and Bob Crosbie drawing the crowds, the games had become the talk of every Saturday.

Alison probably knew as much about football as Harry, she'd been coming to the ground so long. Before they were fifteen, they used to go every Saturday, to watch the first team and the reserves. After the match, they would go back to Harry's house, and cook fried eggs and fried bread, potatoes and baked beans. Harry's mother was usually working, and his grandfather would be down the clubs, celebrating or mourning the latest match, waiting to check the pools. Sitting in the warm kitchen, the table in front of the range, they would eat their tea and listen to Eamonn Andrews on the wireless. While Harry checked his grandfather's coupons, Alison would make the tea, and then they would go to the pictures, sitting close in the back row, giggling at the romantic rubbish and clumsily trying to kiss. In one of the films, Kim Novak was supposed to be married to a famous pianist, and at the end of the film, when he was dying of some terrible illness, he was sitting at the piano playing, and suddenly disappeared. His voice went on talking, telling Kim Novak he was going to be dead. Several people in the cinema were weeping. When Harry looked up and said, 'Where's he gone?' Alison nudged him savagely in the ribs and somebody turned round and told him to be quiet. 'But he's gone,' Harry said again, and an usherette shone her torch in their direction. On his arm, Alison was nearly hysterical, laughing and weeping, thumping him hard with her elbow. In the end, the manager threw them out of the cinema, telling Harry he was disgusting. Every time they went to the cinema now, he said, 'I hope there isn't going to be a pianist,' and Alison was helpless with giggles.

This afternoon the game was tremendous, and the crowds on the terraces went wild, cheering and leaping up and down, yelling with delight every time Bob Crosbie got the ball, screaming at DeGruchy to watch what was going on behind. At every chance of a goal, a mighty roar from twenty thousand voices rose above the stadium and drifted out to sea, where the deckies on the trawlers said you could sometimes hear the noise as far away as the estuary. When a single herring-gull stalked across the middle of the ground, the yells of laughter almost stopped the game, and Bill Evans got a thunder of applause when he pretended to take a kick at the bird and it flew lazily up to the roof of the stadium.

At half time, they had mugs of tea and meat pies that burned their mouths, and when the game ended with the local team winning, Alison threw her arms round Harry's neck and kissed him as if he had scored every goal himself. All around them, people were going wild, hugging each other and slapping strangers on the back, jumping up and down and chanting the name of Town. They poured from the ground singing and shouting for joy, celebrating another victory at the end of the week's work, looking forward to the Saturday evening of pubs and fishermen's clubs, cinemas and noisy dance halls. Even the policemen seemed overjoyed with the afternoon, walking with the crowds out of the ground, chatting with each other about each goal, every move and tactic of the game.

Alison clung tightly to Harry's arm, and when they were out in the main road and walking back towards fishermen's lanes, she stopped and kissed him outside an off-licence, all the blokes going past cheering and slapping Harry on the back, shouting to Alison to have a good time.

The film was *Waterloo Bridge*. Alison seemed cheerful and happy all through their tea, and then as they walked up to the cinema overlooking the promenade, she became quiet, not answering Harry's questions, vague about the things she'd been doing since the floods. He told her about Keith's medical, and how he was getting on at Catterick, but she didn't seem interested. When they got into the cinema, she rested her head on his shoulder, and turned away when he tried to kiss her again. Half-way through the film, he was sure she was crying, but she often cried in films. He thought she enjoyed it.

They walked up to Ted & Blue's afterwards and got some fish and chips. He kept his arm round her, her hair soft on his face. When they'd eaten the food, they sat down in one of the Victorian shelters on the promenade, and watched the lights of the trawlers out on the estuary. Alison sat close in his arms, listening while he told her about the damage the floods had done, the families he knew who'd had to borrow money to pay for new furniture. When she asked about the bait digging, he told her George was thinking of buying a new engine for his boat.

They sat quietly for a long time.

She didn't seem interested in anything he said.

'What is it?' he asked at last, moving to get more comfortable, the hard seats of the shelter pressing into his back.

'What?'

'Summat's wrong.'

'I'm just tired.'

'Too much of books.'

'You always say that.'

'You're always studying.'

She shifted impatiently, and turned to touch his face. Her lips were cold on his cheek, and when she found his mouth, she kissed him hard, pushing her tongue into his mouth and beginning to unfasten his trousers. He flinched when her cold hands touched him, and she pulled away, as if surprised. This was all she would ever do, fumbling inside his trousers. Sometimes, she did it two or three times, leaving him sore and miserable.

He opened his eyes.

'What's the matter?' she said.

'Nothing.'

'I'm not soft, you know.'

'Your hands are cold.'

She sat back, angry.

'I'm sorry.'

'I just said . . .'

'I'm sorry.'

She got up and stood in the door of the shelter. He shivered, waiting for her to sit down. He felt ridiculous, sitting there like that. He couldn't work out what was the matter with her.

'Come on,' he said after a long time, Alison still not moving in the entrance to the shelter.

She shook her head.

'Harry?'

'Yes.'

'Can I ask you something?'

'Go on then. I'll freeze.'

'It's your hands.'

'They're not as cold as yours.'

'It's the digging, I think. The bait. They smell.'

He sat silent for some minutes. She still didn't move. Out at the estuary, the lighthouse blinked across the water. There were no ships in sight.

She came back and sat down again, resting her head on his shoulder and crying, hard, sobbing into his neck. Tears ran down his shirt collar. She put her hand down between his legs and touched him again, half crying, giggling when he groaned. When he came, she kissed him on the mouth, warm and teasing, saying 'I'm sorry, I'm sorry,' as he clung hard to her shoulder.

Far away, they could hear the surf at the tideline. A tram rattled along the top road.

Sleepily, he kept saying Alison's name.

Nine

He saw nothing of Elaine for two or three weeks, and when he went for a drink at the Sunnyside she had already left. Tony had no idea where she was living.

'They don't stay five minutes, these lasses,' he grumbled, banging glasses around angrily at the bar. 'Allus looking for summat else.'

'Maybe you don't pay enough,' Harry shrugged, staring miserably into his beer.

Tony smirked unpleasantly.

'They can earn on the side can't they?' he sniggered.

Arthur was fed up of talking about her.

'You got Alison,' he shouted one night when they were arguing in the Dolphin. 'What the fuck's up with you?'

'Same as you,' Harry shouted back, slamming his beer down on the table.

They sat glaring at each other until Arthur got up and walked out of the pub and Harry was left on his own to finish both drinks. He swallowed them quickly and went for a long walk along the promenade. He kept thinking about Keith, who hadn't been home since his first week at Catterick. He wanted to talk to Alison, but she was always studying during the week. He was lucky if he got to see her at weekends.

Some nights, he cycled down to the promenade and stood listening to the foghorns on the river. There was never anybody about. When they were all at school, they used to meet on the pier most winter nights, except for Wednesdays when the ballroom was opened up for wrestling. Keith was usually there, and a girl called Joanne Mottram who lived in fishermen's lanes with her mother and stepbrother. Joanne liked to sit in the wooden shelter at the end of the pier, smoking Woodbines and laughing at filthy jokes. She had an infectious, croaking laugh and greasy blonde hair, and was notorious at school for grabbing at people in the corridors and following lads into the lavatories if she felt in the mood. She used to hang around on the promenade, but when she found out that Harry and Arthur met on the pier, she started following them. She was married now, to one of the filleters on the fish market. Whenever she saw Harry, she ignored him.

Ronald Timms was the other one who always used to be there. It had been Ronald who first showed them how to use the calcium carbonate. He was always picking on somebody. He was older than the rest of them, fat and white faced but hard from the batterings his father gave him. At school, he had spat a mouthful of pudding into Harry's face on his first day, and when Harry went for him, he kicked him to the ground and smashed his face into the rough concrete, leaving scars for weeks afterwards.

The thing Ronald enjoyed best was organising the tickling benches. The school was divided into two halves, one for boys and one for girls, and a metal railing marked the division in the playground. Wooden benches had been arranged along the railings. Any new boy who refused to hand over his dinner money had to go on these tickling benches, a ritualised assault in which a mob of girls had noisy fun leaning over the railings and grabbing for the underwear of their terrified victims.

Harry remembered a particular girl who always helped Ronald. She had long dark hair and misty, carnal eyes, and was whispered about with some awe by the younger kids. Denise, the older boys said, would let you put your prick right inside her. Harry had no idea what this meant at first, but when Arthur told him she was supposed to let you piss at the same time, he became obsessed with the girl. She left school when she was fourteen, a good seven months pregnant, and Harry went on dreaming about her for years afterwards.

Denise was another one who had married somebody down on the docks, a lumper who worked mainly on the seiners. Harry hadn't seen either of them for years.

When he went to the promenade one night, he saw a light flickering at the end of the pier, and found three bicycles stacked by the ticket office. He could hear voices coming from the shelter at the end of the pier, and recognised Arthur's hard voice immediately. He left his bike by the gate, and walked out to see what they were doing. At the estuary, the warning bell clanged eerily from its buoy. It was freezing cold, a thick fog drifting in off the estuary, foghorns moaning and wailing across the banks. The slatted boards were wet and slippery with the fog, and he could hear the sea underneath sucking and slapping against the iron struts.

Arthur was kneeling at one of the benches, moulding bread into small pellets. When he saw Harry, he nodded and concentrated on what he was doing.

At the railings, Elaine was smoking a cigarette.

Danny Sellwood was sitting in the shelter, watching.

'What's he doing here?' Harry asked, nodding towards Danny.

Elaine shrugged.

'I found him in town,' she said quietly. 'We were having a cup of tea.'

'I told her Danny's the only girl allowed on this pier,' Arthur said with a nod towards Elaine. 'That right, Danny?'

Danny said nothing, and Arthur laughed aloud, pleased with himself. He'd been in a foul mood for days, ever since his brother Patrick got back from the Arctic. Patrick was taking a trip off, and that always meant rows and fights. He brought money into the house, and showed off with his flash clothes. He kept sneering at Arthur for working down on the docks.

'What you up to, Arthur?' Harry asked.

'Nothing.'

'You've not got that rubbish with you, have you?'

53

'Fuck off, Harry.'

'I'll not let you.'

'I said fuck off.'

Arthur glanced at him furiously, still moulding the pellets, and then looked round at Elaine.

'You still here?' he said, his voice flat and hard.

Elaine just laughed and blew smoke cheerfully into his face.

'Shove off yourself, Arthur,' she grinned, lounging back against the railings.

Harry sat down on the bench beside Danny and lit a cigarette.

It was too much trouble to bother with Arthur.

He took a long drag at the cigarette and offered the packet to Danny.

They called Danny potato head at school because of his big round face and shining eyes. He must be seventeen now, but he looked no older than twelve. He lived with his mother behind the sweetshop opposite Thrunscoe school. His father had gone to Birmingham to find work and ended up living with another woman and her child. You could make Danny cry, asking him when his father was coming home. Harry's mother worked in the sweetshop briefly, but she couldn't stand Danny hanging around. He upset her. Harry had been there for tea when Mrs Sellwood was trying to persuade his mother to stay. She could never get anybody to work for her for long on the money the shop could afford. Kids crowded into the shop after school and stole sweets while she was trying to serve.

At the railings, Elaine lit another cigarette.

'You didn't come that Sunday,' Harry said, and she looked puzzled, pushing her hair out of her eyes. Her hair was damp and curling at the forehead. She was wearing a thin grey coat and a white blouse. She looked cold.

'Come?'

'Down the prom. I was going to show you Happiland.'

'Oh,' she shrugged, smiling and watching Arthur. 'You know.'

Arthur had finished what he was doing and stood up and clapped his hands.

'Right,' he said, pleased with himself. 'That's it then.'

He took a torch out of his pocket and flicked the switch. The beam dazzled Harry's eyes, and he held his hands up to his face. Going to the railings, Arthur pushed Elaine to one side and shone the torch up to the roof of the pier.

'Do you have to?' Harry muttered, but Arthur took no notice.

The beam of the torch shone straight up into the darkness. Arthur circled it slowly in a wide arc, and they could hear the gulls stirring up on the roof. He waited until a dozen herring-gulls lifted off the green ridge tiles and flew into the beam of the light, and then tossed handfuls of the pellets out into the darkness. As the birds screamed and squabbled after the bread, diving down to the sea, he switched the torch off and told everybody to keep quiet. They stood in the darkness, listening to the slow flap of wings, the distant moan of foghorns from the trawlers out at the estuary. Beneath the pier, the tide washed icily against the shore.

After several seconds, there was a muffled, spluttering explosion, and bits of feather and blood suddenly hit Harry in the face. He jumped and cursed Arthur. A second later, there was another explosion, and then four or five in rapid succession, shattering the winter silence.

When Elaine screamed, Harry leapt up and found her in the darkness. Arthur was laughing. Harry put his arm round Elaine's shoulders and she pressed her face into his coat, shivering as Arthur turned the torch on. When Harry looked at her, her face was white with shock.

'That was a bloody stupid thing to do,' Harry shouted angrily, glaring at Arthur.

'Fuck off, Harry.'

'You could have done just one.'

'I said fuck off.'

In the shelter, Danny suddenly stood up, his big moon grin beaming at them in the torchlight.

'Birds,' he said, smiling at Arthur. 'Birds.'

Arthur stared at him nastily. He spat at the railings, a gob of phlegm shivering from the flaked paint before falling into the sea.

'Birds,' Danny repeated.

Arthur stared at him viciously.

'You all right, potato head?' he sneered.

'Potato head.'

'Fucking potato head.'

Harry could feel Arthur working himself up. He wanted Danny to say something stupid. He wanted to hit out at somebody. As Arthur took a step forward, Elaine grabbed Danny's arm and pulled him back towards the seats. She glared at Arthur, and held on to Danny's arm.

'You leave him alone,' she said angrily, and then forced a quick smile. 'You leave him alone.'

For a moment, Arthur stood and stared at her, and then suddenly he kicked out at the wooden bench and knocked what was left of the bread to the floor. His eyes were white with fury. He was trembling. He kicked the seat again and again, shouting furiously.

'You want to feed the seagulls, potato head?' he yelled, grabbing on the floor for the remainder of the pellets. 'You want to feed the fucking seagulls?'

He got some of the pellets into his hand and made a lunge for Danny. Bread scattered across the wooden boards. Elaine jumped up and stood in front of him. Her hair was wet through with the fog. Her cheeks were bright red. She pushed Arthur angrily in the chest, sending him reeling back against the railings.

'No,' she shouted, her voice rough with panic. 'No, you don't. No.'

Harry told Danny they had to go. He said his mother would be waiting for him. Danny got up to leave the shelter straight away.

'You must be off your head, Arthur,' Harry said as he followed him.

'Sod off, Harry.'

'You coming, Elaine?'

'In a minute.'

As they walked down the pier, he could hear Elaine crying.

He wanted to turn back and fetch her but he had to get Danny home.

His hands were shaking.

They rode back through the town, the fog closing round them so that they could hardly see, the streetlights glowing eerily in the bitter cold.

At the shop, Mrs Sellwood was waiting in the passage.

'Where have you been?' she cried when she saw Daniel.

When she saw Harry she was excited and flustered, thanking him and saying she was going to put the kettle on. Danny told Harry he wanted to show him something in his room. There was no carpet on the stairs. Harry followed him, stumbling on a broken rail. Danny opened his bedroom door and showed him inside. The walls were covered with pictures and photographs cut from magazines. They were all of the same actress, Doris Day. She smiled at them from every wall, her eyes an intense blue, her hair dazzling blonde. Danny beamed round at his collection. When Harry said nothing, he went over to his record player and took a record from the rack beside the bed. He put the record on and it spun on the turntable with a steady hiss. It was Doris Day, 'Once, I Had a Secret Love'. Standing in the small bedroom, surrounded by the smiling faces, Harry listened to the song. When it was finished, he said he had to go.

Outside in the cold, Harry got on to his bike and Danny stood shivering on the pavement.

'See you then,' Harry muttered, the wind freezing his damp shirt to his back.

'Can we go again?' Danny said, his hand resting on Harry's handlebars.

'What?'

'To see Elaine. I like Elaine.'

Harry could see Mrs Sellwood in the doorway, peering down the passage.

'We don't go that often,' he said.

'But when you do?'

'Yes, if you like.'

'To the pier?'

'Yes.'

As Harry cycled up the road, he could hear Danny shouting through the fog. At the corner, he looked back, and he was still there, standing outside the shop, waving both arms.

By the time he got back to the pier, Elaine and Arthur had gone.

Ten

Maintenance work on the fairgrounds usually began in March, ready for the Easter opening. The floods had changed that. The smaller stalls and shops with plate glass windows had suffered the most damage, needing extensive rebuilding. The bigger fairgrounds and amusement arcades fitted new doors and shutters and brought mechanics down to the promenade to get the repairs done throughout January and February. It was the machinery and rides that had taken the worst of the damage. Hardly any stock was kept during the winter, but the fairground equipment couldn't be moved and had been badly knocked about and dented. Whenever Harry saw Mac, he was grumbling about the cost, but it wasn't the sort of work where Harry could be of any help.

On a Saturday morning when he had no work on for George Bainbridge, Harry went down to the promenade and dumped his bicycle outside Happiland. It was a cold, clear morning, the sky brilliant blue over the sea, the sun warm on his face. Several stallholders were already busy, and shouted hello as Harry cycled along the wide promenade. From radios and juke boxes, music drifted out towards the deserted sands. A man was walking along the foreshore, throwing a stick for his dog which ran in enormous circles, yapping at the excited gulls.

Mac was already busy at Happiland, helping Les Tunstall oil the machinery of the bigger rides and games.

'Late as usual,' Les grinned, his thin face like a rat's peering from behind the row of bagatelle tables.

Mac waved the oil can in the air.

'You ready for work, Harry?' he shouted, and then ducked down again behind the counter before Harry could answer.

'Building work all finished?' Harry said, glancing round the empty fairground.

'Cost me a fortune,' Mac replied. 'Cost me a bloody fortune.'

They were working on the grand national race, an electrified horse race with the horses in individual tracks banked steeply on a wooden stand against a wall. The punters sat at bagatelle tables in front of the race, and every time they scored at the bagatelle game, their horse was jerked forward on its electric cable.

It was Harry's favourite game. You could sit down all day when you were looking after the grand national race, using the microphone and chatting with the crowds. If you wanted a particular horse to win, usually one being played by some girl in a hooped skirt and low-necked, flare-sleeved blouse, all you had to do was tighten the electric cable. The prizes were sugar bowls and teddy bears and huge plastic dolls wearing peroxide wigs and purple underwear.

Harry liked working for Mac.

He was a sentimental, shrewd man, overweight and bald as a seagull, puffy-eyed with a white unhealthy skin. During the summer months, he hardly ever saw any sunlight. Harry had driven with him to Hull once or twice to buy cheap lots of prizes, crockery with gold rims and loud patterns of grapes and exotic flowers, gold-plated lamps with naked breasts on transparent shades. When Harry's mother came down to the fairground one Sunday afternoon, Mac made sure she won first prize on the grand national race, an enormous teddy bear with *Seconds* stamped behind his ear.

Mac finished behind the bagatelle tables and stood up, sweat pouring down his round face.

'I had a terrible winter,' he said melodramatically. 'Everything going wrong. You looking for work, Harry?'

'You know I am.'

'Never take a man for granted. You want to make some tea, Les?'

'I'm doing this, ent I?'

'Don't exhaust your possibilities.'

Walking round to the front of the race, Mac slapped Harry cheerfully on the shoulder and wrapped his arm round him.

'Am I glad to see you, boy. And what about your criminal friend, Arthur?'

'He's working down the docks, Mac. On the barrows.'

'God help the fish merchants. He not in the army yet?'

Les sniggered, hearing this.

'They've got some standards,' he said. 'He'll be on the boats by this autumn, you see.'

'Come and drink tea,' Mac sighed, squeezing Harry's arm.

Behind the race was Mac's small office where he did his accounts and brewed the tea. The race was on the right-hand wall of the fairground, next to Wonderland. Beyond Mac's office, at the back of Happiland, was a large area that had been roped off and set aside for the juke box. There were wooden benches round the walls, and for threepence, couples could stand or sit in the hot darkness, clinging together and swaying to the loud music, heavy-petting to the thump of the records. When you sat in Mac's office, you could hear the boom of the music, vibrating through the concrete walls.

'How'm I going to manage, Harry?' Mac groaned when he had filled the kettle and plugged it into the wall. 'I'm still recovering from those damned floods.'

'So are a lot of people, Mac.'

'And me with no insurance!'

'I don't believe you,' Harry said.

'No insurance at all. You still drink it like tar?'

Mac never missed a thing.

When Harry and Arthur started working on the fair-grounds, during school holidays, they learnt every trick there was to make extra money. In the change kiosks you could put eleven pennies instead of twelve into the small piles of change customers needed for the slot machines. On the fruit machines, it was possible to alter the balances so that the jackpots couldn't be won, and then clear the machines out when nobody was looking. On the waltzer and the cages-of-death, if you checked the floor after every ride you usually found silver coins in the dust. As the crowds got drunker throughout the day, it was easier to take their money, but as long as you weren't ripping him off, Mac didn't seem to care. He kept watching, but he never said a word.

'You want full-time?' Mac said now, drinking his tea and wiping the top of his head with his silk handkerchief.

'Bit of bait digging occasionally. Not much.'

'And signing on,' Mac grinned.

'How about Monday?' Harry asked. 'I could make a start on the dodgems?'

'Perfect. Les can look after the big dipper. He'll enjoy that.'

Harry finished his tea and went back out into the fairground, leaving Mac staring unhappily at a pile of invoices. Les was still busy working on the grand national race.

Harry walked the length of the fairground, looking at all the rides and games, enjoying the strange excitement he always felt when he was in Happiland. Along the back wall of the fairground, alternating with the rifle range, coconut shy and darts stall, were the ghost train, haunted house and hall of mirrors. The stock-rooms were behind these games: a series of musty rooms with barred windows overlooking the railway lines. At the far end of the fairground, on the wall facing the grand national race, were the candy floss and rock stalls, and a new hot-dog bar that Pete Brown's sister was going to try and run. The big rides were arranged in the centre of the fairground: the waltzer and dodgems and cages-of-death, the rocket rides and the golden gallopers. Banks of fruit machines were grouped all over the fairground, and change kiosks so that customers wouldn't have to stop playing. At the very front of the huge building, open to the promenade, were the laughing policeman and drunken sailor, the fortune teller and lucky dips, and two separate games of housey-housey. The big dipper was outside, standing between Happiland and Wonderland.

Harry enjoyed wandering around. Most of the rides were still sheeted down with tarpaulin. Seagulls rustled and flapped up above in the darkness, perching on the huge rafters. Outside the fairground, the sea glinted in warm sunlight.

'Can't wait to start,' he told Les when he got back to the grand national race.

'You must be daft.'

'It's great. *You* come every year.'

'Nowt else, is there,' Les said sarcastically.

Shouting goodbye to Mac, Harry walked back along the promenade, wheeling his bike in the sunlight, breathing the cold air. At the novelty gift shop, Andrea Walters was unloading painted seashells out of the back of her car, and stopped to ask Harry how he was getting on. He helped her move some of the boxes of shells into the shop, and then walked on to Mildred's café, hoping she would be open. During the season, he always had his lunch at Mildred's, and according to Arthur, Elaine had just got herself a job there.

'I saw her on the tram,' Arthur said when he asked him how he knew.

They never talked about the night with the herring-gulls.

When Harry got to the café, Mildred was busy checking stock behind the counter.

'Well, you're a fine one,' she shouted when he opened the door. 'Not coming to say hello.'

'I'm here, aren't I?'

'I should think so 'n' all.'

Coming round from the counter, Mildred gave Harry a big hug and nearly broke his back. She was a huge woman, with broad shoulders and heavy arms. Her voice boomed in the little café, and she held Harry by the shoulders, examining his face as if she hadn't seen him for years.

'You're looking well,' she grinned, 'I'll say that. How's that lovely mother of yours?'

'She's fine, Mildred.'

'And Jack?'

63

'They're both great. Recovering from the floods.'

'Was it bad?' Mildred asked seriously.

'Not too bad. Jack bought us new furniture and stuff.'

'Bless him.'

'Any chance of a bacon buttie?'

Mildred laughed loudly and released his arms, going back behind the counter and shouting through to the stock-room.

'I got a new girl,' she said to Harry. 'Going to be helping Margaret.'

Elaine came through to the counter and stood in the doorway, smiling at Harry. She had the dress on she'd been wearing the night he saw her at the Sunnyside. The sleeves were rolled up, and she was holding a yellow duster.

'This is Elaine,' Mildred was saying, winking at Harry.

'We've met,' Elaine said, looking embarrassed.

Mildred raised her eyebrows.

'Oh?'

'When I was working at the Sunnyside,' Elaine explained. 'He came in for a drink.'

'Did he?' Mildred nodded, staring happily at Harry.

'Any chance of that buttie?' Harry asked again.

Mildred laughed.

'I thought you always ate at Peter's,' she said mischievously.

'I'm too hungry to walk that far,' he grinned.

'I bet you are, you lazy sod.'

While Mildred fried the bacon and chatted about the coming season, Harry sat in the window and smoked a cigarette. Elaine went back into the stock-room. The man with the dog was walking back along the foreshore, hands deep in his pockets, kicking at the sand. Mildred hummed and grumbled about the cost of supplies, brewing the kettle for some tea, and when she'd finished, shouted to Elaine to come and give Harry his meal.

'You stay in here,' she said. 'I'll finish in the stock-room.'

Bringing the food across to his table, Elaine sat down and watched him eat, wiping her forehead with her arm.

'You haven't got a cigarette, have you?' she smiled. 'I'm right out.'

'You know I have.'

'Thanks.'

While she lit the cigarette, he drank the tea and took a mouthful of hot bacon.

'Arthur said you were working here,' he told her.

'Oh yes?'

'He said he met you on a tram?'

'That's right.'

She stared vaguely out of the window.

In the stock-room, Mildred was busy sorting boxes for the shelves. On the wireless, they were playing Fats Domino's 'Ain't That a Shame'.

'You want to go to the pictures, Elaine?' Harry asked, pushing his plate away and stubbing his cigarette out in the ashtray.

'Tonight?'

'Yes, if you like.'

'I'm going out. One of the salesmen asked me. Come in here this morning. I don't know where we're going.'

'Tomorrow then. They change the programme tomorrow.'

'Got to see my mum and dad. Won't be time once we get busy, Mildred says. I'm living in. Sharing with that Margaret. You know her?'

Margaret was the woman who usually worked in the café. She was a dark-haired, sour woman, a Roman Catholic who was always talking about sin. She had bad spots and made Harry feel uncomfortable.

'She talks in her sleep,' Elaine said. 'About men. Wakes me up. I can't stand sharing.'

'Maybe next week then?' Harry said.

'If you like.'

'I usually have my lunch here,' Harry told her, fastening his coat and pushing his chair back from the table.

'Thanks for the cigarette.'

She went back behind the counter and got a bucket and

mop to start cleaning the floors. Harry paid Mildred for the lunch and said he would be in on Monday. As he left the café, Elaine was working by the door, and he had to push past her. She smiled, moving the bucket aside. He had gone half-way down the promenade before he remembered his bicycle, leaning outside the café windows.

Eleven

Upstairs the toilet flushed for the second time and Harry's mother bit her lip, trying not to tip the frying pan.

'Take no notice of him,' she giggled as she put the bacon and eggs and fried bread out on plates. 'He doesn't mean anything.'

Upstairs, Jack slammed the bathroom door and after a second, they heard his bedroom door shut with a thud. He had a thick green curtain behind the door to keep his room warm, and the curtain deadened the sound of his coughing and slamming about.

Sitting down at the table, Harry's mother poured herself a cup of tea and sighed.

'You forget he's old sometimes.'

'He's not old,' Harry laughed.

'He's eighty-two, Harry.'

'He'll live for ever,' Harry grinned, munching his food and knocking the bottom of the sauce bottle to get some more out. 'What's up with him this morning, anyway?'

'Mrs Blakey asked him to go to the Old Tyme Dancing.'

'What, opposite the Winter Gardens?'

'Café Dansant,' Harry's mother laughed, imitating Mrs Blakey's false accent. 'He told her he wasn't old enough.'

'I bet it was the two-shilling entrance charge he was worried about,' Harry said. 'He's no romance.'

In his bedroom, Jack was going through his morning ritual of coughing his heart out and Harry's mother raised her eyebrows.

'Cigarettes,' she said bitterly. 'He must have smoked half he earned over the years.'

Harry finished his breakfast and rinsed his plate under the cold tap. In the yard, the sunlight was already warm and the neighbour's cat was stalking along the top of the fence, staring coldly up at a flock of starlings.

'Did you hear about Mrs Goddard, Harry?' his mother asked.

'What about her?'

'She's ever so upset.'

'Why?'

'They thought Keith was going to get exemption.'

'I don't see why.'

'He's never been very strong.'

Harry shrugged.

'She's been ill,' his mother went on. 'I saw her in the market. She misses him, I expect.'

Harry boiled a kettle up and filled the sink with hot water. He washed the plates and then boiled another kettle for a flask. Upstairs, Jack's bedroom door banged open, and a second later they heard the toilet flushing again.

'That was a quick one,' Harry grinned, getting his coat from behind the door.

The toilet seat went with a crash for the third time.

'I'm glad it's wood,' his mother sighed, and getting up, kissed Harry briefly on the cheek as he went off to work.

Harry spent all morning putting an undercoat on the green shutters at the front of Happiland. Mac had gone to London to do some business, and Les had cleared off after his second cup of tea. He was going to see some friends in the clubs, he told Harry, which meant he would be spending all day going round the drinking clubs on the docks. If he was lucky, he would get free drinks all day, and come back tomorrow with a foul hangover.

The sun was warm on Harry's back as he worked. There were several trawlers out at the estuary and on the river, and the promenade was busy with fairground people working on the amusements and waiting for deliveries of stocks for the Easter opening. Van-loads of rock and candy floss powder, cheap gifts and prizes would be arriving every day from now on, and Harry loved the excitement and bustle. He worked steadily the whole length of the fairground, getting a good thick undercoating done, thinking about his grandfather as he worked.

There were photographs of Harry's grandparents on the mantelpiece and in his mother's bedroom, but the photograph he liked best was one Jack carried in his wallet. It showed the couple standing outside the Congregational Chapel down on the docks. There were sailing smacks in the background, lined up at the north wall where the trawlers were moored ready for departure. Jack looked in a bad mood even then, as if he was impatient to get off to sea. Harry's grandmother was smiling into the camera, squinting into brilliant sunlight. The photograph was taken in 1910, the year they were married.

'Perfect marriage we had,' Jack always used to say when he was feeling sentimental. 'She was a good woman, your grandmother. I don't know why she had to be taken from me.'

Harry's mother always laughed when he went on like this, but there were usually tears in her eyes. She could remember her mother clearly. A tall, energetic woman, she said, working in the curing houses and struggling to keep the tiny house clean. She died when Harry's mother was seven, in 1926, the year of the big strike.

'She came from Aberdeen they say,' Harry's mother once told him. 'With the fishergirls. Used to travel down the coast from Scotland, following the herring fleets. Gutting quines, they called them round here. Don't ask me why she married your grandfather.'

Harry liked it when his mother told him things about the past, about the fishing and their family. When he was still at primary school, she used to sit with him beside the range and read to him, toasting muffins on a fork over the fire. He remembered the feel of her hair, soft and tickling against his face, and her eyes, shining in the flames of the fire.

He could remember nothing really pleasant about his grandfather.

He went to Mildred's for his lunch, but Elaine was visiting her parents.

'Won't be a chance after next weekend,' Mildred told him. 'Rushed off our feet, we shall be.'

'You hope so.'

They both laughed. Mildred lived in a big house not far from the promenade. She had no husband. The girls lived in when they worked for Mildred, sleeping in a small room above the kitchens. Mildred had a son in a private school, but they never saw him down on the promenade.

It was gone four when Arthur cycled down to Happiland and wheeled his bike into the fairground. A cold mist was blowing in off the sea and Harry had finished a good topcoat of green gloss. He was washing the brushes. Arthur looked cold and tired, and while Harry finished cleaning the brushes, Arthur drank what was left in the flask, flicking lumps of chocolate to a stray dog that had followed him into the fairground.

'Thirty ships this morning,' he grumbled, his face drained of colour, his eyes dark with fatigue. 'Lumpers were playing hell.'

'Their job's easy enough.'

'Tell them that, Harry.'

The lumpers had to unload the ships for the market, starting at two o'clock in the morning. The auction began at seven-thirty. It was a Dutch auction, the auctioneer starting with a high price and everybody waiting to risk how low it would go. If there were a lot of ships with good catches, the market price would drop, but the lumpers would still have to work hard to get everything ready. That was when the backhanders started, to keep everybody happy. Working on the barrows, nobody ever thought to give Arthur a backhander. He had to earn his extra money stealing fish.

Elaine came in just as Harry was drying the brushes.

She was wearing a cheap coat and high-heeled shoes. She

shivered, sitting down on one of the bagatelle stools at the grand national race.

'Is it allus this cold?' she grumbled, opening her handbag and searching for a cigarette.

'Soon be summer,' Harry laughed.

He shook the brushes out and smiled at Elaine.

'Your parents all right?'

'Why shouldn't they be?'

Harry went to put the paint things in one of the stockrooms, and when he got back, Elaine was feeding the stray dog pieces of Arthur's chocolate.

'How's Mildred?' he asked, sitting down on one of the stools.

'Stupid woman,' Elaine scowled.

'Mildred's all right.'

'She doesn't have to sleep with a religious maniac,' Elaine said nastily. 'I think I should have a separate bedroom.'

'Tell her,' Arthur said.

'You tell her.'

'Nowt to do with me,' Arthur said, staring at her in surprise. 'I don't care where you sleep.'

'Oh no?'

Harry leaned back against the bagatelle table and yawned.

'Nowt like a laugh,' he grinned at Arthur.

'Is that meant for me?'

'Eat your chocolate, Elaine.'

'It's for the dog.'

'Give it to the dog then. We're not stopping you.'

Kneeling down on the concrete floor, she let the dog lick her fingers, giving it what was left of the chocolate. When the chocolate was finished, she got up and brushed past Arthur, going over to the golden gallopers. Lifting her skirt, she climbed up on to the nearest horse and sat there, kicking her legs. The dog followed her and watched, looking up and patiently waiting for more chocolate.

'All gone,' she said smiling down at the dog. 'Can you start this?'

'We're not open.'

'Mean.'

'There's no power.'

'Mean. I'd do it for you.'

'There's no power.'

Leaning forward, she swung lazily on the horse, hanging on to the elaborately painted saddle. The horse's eyes shone in the overhead lighting. Harry was frozen, sitting at the bagatelle tables. Arthur stood slumped against the change kiosk, staring at the ground.

'You could push?' Elaine said with a smile. 'Two strong fellers like you.'

'I've been pushing all fucking day,' Arthur grinned.

'Won't take much,' she said.

Harry glanced at Arthur. He shrugged, and they walked across to the golden gallopers.

'I'm ever so easy to push,' Elaine said, smiling down at them. At their feet, the dog looked up at the girl, its mouth wide open, its tongue lolling out.

They got behind the horse and started to push the great heavy roundabout. It was solid wood and steel, with a massive engine at the centre for turning the horses, but the platform the horses were actually on wasn't so heavy. Kicking her legs, Elaine giggled and urged them on. Gradually, the ride began to move. Harry felt the sweat forming on his face, his hands blistering. He pushed harder, and the horses began to move. The dog barked excitedly.

'Go on,' Elaine shouted, slapping the sides of the horse she was on. 'Go on, go on.'

Behind him, Harry could hear Arthur cursing. They put all their strength into the effort, the horses very suddenly beginning to move faster, Elaine's skirt brushing against Harry's face, the dog yapping and running round after them.

'It's lovely, it's lovely,' Elaine shouted. 'Keep going, go on, keep going.'

Harry could hear Arthur giggling. They were both laughing. The dog snapped at their feet and up in the gloomy rafters seagulls were screaming and flapping about, disturbed by the sudden noise. In the great empty fairground, the golden gallopers raced beneath the lights, painted harnesses and big eyes shining as the ride turned, Elaine's excitement echoing round the deserted fairground.

'Don't stop, don't stop,' she kept shouting, but Arthur collapsed on to the ground, helpless with laughter, and Harry felt himself being carried round with the ride. Letting go, he reached for the legs of one of the horses, and lifted himself up on to the wooden floor. He nearly slipped as the dog went for his feet. Arthur sat on the floor, shaking with laughter. Climbing up on to the horse behind Elaine, Harry clung desperately to the saddle, his arms aching from all the pushing, his head dizzy with the speed of the ride. He closed his eyes, and heard Elaine singing. 'Ain't That a Shame,' she was singing, her voice sweet and pure in the empty fairground, the dog following her howling as she spun round and round. Then 'Only You' as the golden gallopers slowed down, her voice lovely and clear, echoing up to the dark rafters.

When they stopped, she turned round and smiled at him.

'Don't stop, don't stop,' Arthur mimicked on the floor, his face wet with tears.

In its excitement, the dog seemed to be in a frenzy.

Twelve

It was the hottest opening weekend they'd had for years.

On the Saturday, thousands of trippers poured into the resort. On the station, trains pulled into the platforms from early in the morning until the middle of the afternoon. Buses queued up for parking places in the car parks. The hotels and guest houses had 'No Vacancies' signs up before the weekend had even begun.

Harry was exhausted by the end of the day.

The engine on the grand national race fused, the pellets for the rifle range were the wrong size, the powder filter on the candy floss machine got clogged with damp powder. From ten in the morning until gone midnight, Harry rushed round the fairground with Mac, keeping the change kiosks supplied with coins, helping sort out the mechanical problems, rushing into town to buy any spare parts they'd forgotten. By the time he got to bed, his feet were aching and his head throbbed with the music and crowds, and the sweltering heat inside the covered fairground.

'You don't know what heat is,' Norman Tattelin boasted when Harry got to the fairground on the Sunday morning.

Mac and Les were already busy handing out cash for the change kiosks, and Norman was boasting to the new lad about how he kept fit all winter. Norman Tattelin was the fairground bouncer. He had spent years in the army in India. His face was mottled and bright red, and he had a sandy moustache and bulging eyes. He was in his forties and lived in digs behind the railway station where he washed his one shirt every night and hung it over the bath to dry. He didn't know how to use an iron. By the end of each day, the collar of his shirt would be black with sweat and grime.

Harry's first job in Happiland, the year he started working for Mac, had been to fetch Norman's beer.

'Good lad,' he used to say, giving Harry half a crown each time he made the trip to the pub. He also got to keep the returns money.

Norman wore thick cavalry-twill trousers and his check shirt regardless of the heat.

'You had a good winter, lad?' He beamed at Harry, punching him savagely on the arm.

'Give over, Norman.'

'You're not fit, lad. This is Clive. Harry's been here for years, Clive. He's waiting for his national service papers.'

The new lad was tall and fair-haired. He had expensive clothes on. When Norman introduced them he held his hand out and shook Harry's hand cheerfully. He had a hard grip.

'You from round here?' Harry asked.

'No.'

'He's on the dodge.' Norman winked, shaking his head. 'No idea, you youngsters. Finest life in the world, the army, and he's on the dodge.'

Harry looked again at the new lad. They'd had national service dodgers before, lads moving from fairground to building site to keep ahead of the police, working on the fairgrounds for a few weeks and then disappearing at the first sign of the police. Mac didn't usually take them on. They were too much trouble. At least they weren't claiming the dole like half the blokes on the fairgrounds, but just when you'd taught them a job, they'd be gone.

Norman didn't like it. No matter how friendly he seemed.

By lunch-time, the fairground was getting busy. In the tremendous heat, families stayed down on the sands, swimming and fooling around in the sea, eating sandwiches and ice creams and watching the Punch & Judy shows and the big wheel and scenic railway. Above the noise of the rides and games and fairground machinery, you could still hear the roar of the crowds out on the beaches, children shrieking and grown-ups splashing in the shallow water, gulls wheeling and crying above the crowds, the waves pounding up the burning sands.

Harry showed Clive how to handle the microphone on the housey-housey tables and the grand national race.

'It's just chat, really,' he said. 'Be friendly, keep 'em happy. They like a good time. And make sure you keep the money in the bag.'

Everybody working on the fairground had a leather shoulder-bag slung over their shoulder and hanging down in front of them. Mac and Norman went round periodically, collecting any bigger coins or notes. All you needed for change were pennies for the slot machines. Harry's hands were green within a couple of hours of arriving, and the sweat was beginning to run down his face. He was wearing old trousers and a thin shirt, and heavy boots. On the concrete floor, if you wore plimsolls, you could hardly walk by the end of the day.

The crowds began to pack the fairground during the afternoon.

A gang of Teds came down, wearing electric-green socks, jackets with velvet collars, drainpipe trousers and brothel-creepers, the shoes with thick crêpe soles. They paraded round Happiland like a fashion show, flicking combs through their hair and shouting to all the girls. Older people stood and laughed at them and Les said they looked like a bunch of queers. Furious, Norman followed them round, hoping they'd do something he could get upset about.

'He likes fighting,' Harry explained to Clive. 'He'd do this job for nothing.'

There were fights most nights on the promenade, Norman weighing in like a drunken bull, causing more trouble than he stopped, throwing savage punches with an accuracy you wouldn't have believed, considering the amount of beer he put away. Mac used to stand and watch him with an aggrieved frown, muttering that he was more trouble than he was worth. But he never offered to sack him.

All afternoon, heat blistered the metal roof; rocket rides

and dodgems and the waltzer screamed and thundered in the huge enclosed space, thousands of punters jostled and shrieked and spent money – a mass of kiss-me-quick hats and Hawaiian shirts, florid complexions and overweight, sweating grandmothers and excited, frantic children.

The Teds came and played a game on the grand national race, a dozen of them with DA hairstyles and metal combs, jeering at Harry and banging the bagatelle tables to try and win, applauding loudly when one of their gang won an enormous golliwog. Most of them were still at school, or waiting to go in the army.

'Fucking layabouts,' Norman grumbled when Harry sat down with him for tea. They got half an hour for lunch, and two twenty-minute breaks which they could take when they liked. Harry always saved his breaks for late afternoon and evening. By the end of the day, he needed a rest.

'They're only kids,' Harry said, and Norman roared with laughter, choking on his tea and spilling some down his shirt. He was wearing an army tie, spotted with grease stains and sweat.

'They are,' Harry protested, closing his eyes and resting his head back against the concrete wall of Mac's office. 'They're still at school, most of 'em.'

'Listen to the old man of the sea,' Norman grinned.

Collapsing on another seat, Pete Brown's sister groaned at the pain in her feet and asked if there was any tea left in the pot.

'You're not fit, Brenda,' Norman explained pompously. 'What you want to do . . .'

'What I want to do is go to sleep, Norman Tattelin,' Brenda told him crossly. 'A cup of tea will have to do in the meantime.'

'I'm only trying to explain . . .'

'Go and beat somebody up, will you, you great daft pillock.'

Outside on the promenade the illuminations were shining on the sea. Thousands of people were still out in the warm air, enjoying the evening, excited by the lights and music, the heat and noise. In Happiland, everything was alight, the rides packed with screaming holidaymakers, the dodgems crashing and thumping on their electric cables, the waltzer and rocket rides whirling round and round with thousands of coloured light-bulbs shimmering in the brilliant darkness.

Harry felt the excitement.

At his side, Mac was grumbling about what all this electricity was costing him. Over by the haunted house, Norman was arguing with a couple of drunken fishermen, threatening them with a good belt. On the golden gallopers, a crowd of louts were yelling abuse at the queues waiting for the horses.

Harry was tired out, but he never wanted the days to end.

He dreaded the end of the season, when the fairgrounds closed down for the winter. Apart from the bait digging, there had never been anything else he wanted to do. He couldn't imagine any work suiting him better.

At nine o'clock, he saw Alison and one of her friends talking to Clive Smalley.

'I hate this town,' Alison was saying when he walked up to them. 'I can't wait to get away.'

'It's all right,' Clive shrugged. 'You get used to places.'

'You are lucky, living down south.'

'You want a candy floss, Alison?' Harry grinned, kissing her cheek and taking her arm.

'Lovely,' her friend giggled.

'And a toffee apple,' Alison insisted. 'We must have a toffee apple.'

'Don't forget the hot-dogs,' Clive grinned.

He went off to help at the fruit machines, and Harry walked with the girls to the front of the fairground. He paid for the candy floss and toffee apples and they stood outside in the warm evening air, the tide right up to the breakers now, the waves washing gently up the sands and the lights of trawlers bobbing up and down at the estuary.

'I've never seen such crowds,' Alison's friend chattered. 'You are lucky, working down here.'

'Don't you live in town then?' Harry asked, surprised.

'In a village a few miles out. My parents never let me come down here. Not like Alison. You are lucky, Alison, with your parents.'

'That's what you think,' Alison frowned, licking her candy floss. 'This stuff is foul. It's all sticky.'

'It's supposed to be sticky,' Harry laughed.

He looked at Alison, and she blushed, frowning and licking her lips.

'When are you going to get a proper job, Harry?' she said cleverly, showing off in front of her friend.

'This is a proper job.'

'No it isn't.'

'Good money,' Harry pointed out.

'Well, I think he's lucky,' Alison's friend interrupted. 'I wish I could work down here.'

'Before going to college,' Harry laughed.

'Yes.'

'Is that what you're doing, Harry?' Alison said in her exaggerated voice, mocking him. 'I didn't realise that.'

'Where are you going?' the other girl asked. 'I'm going to Nottingham, I hope. That will be fun.'

Harry shrugged and dropped the rest of his toffee apple into one of the rubbish bins on the pavement.

'Got to get back,' he explained, smiling at Alison. 'Don't get too sticky. See you around.'

'You'll be lucky,' Alison shouted, annoyed with him for walking away.

'But he's lovely,' he heard Alison's friend say as he pushed back into the crowds.

'So are you,' he shouted, but he could see they hadn't heard him.

Back on the waltzer, where he was due to relieve Andrew in the ticket box, he watched Alison and her friend leave the fairground, and he knew they would be back tomorrow.

Thirteen

'She's horrible,' Margaret said, banging Harry's plate down in front of him. 'She tells lies about me. She shouldn't be allowed to do that.'

'Give her a belt in the mouth, I should,' Arthur joked, covering his chips with tomato sauce.

'Take no notice, Margaret,' Harry said.

'She's doing it all the time, telling Mildred I say things.'

'Say things?' Harry said.

'In my sleep.'

'What things?' Arthur grinned, looking interested.

'About men.'

'Margaret!'

'I don't. It's all lies.'

'How do you know?'

'It's all lies.'

'I mean, if you're asleep,' Arthur munched through his chips, waving his fork in the air and nodding seriously, 'I don't see how you could know.'

'Margaret!'

Mildred's hard voice made them all jump, and Harry nearly choked on a chip, Arthur getting up elaborately and slapping him on the back.

'Have a drink,' he advised solemnly. 'We'll go down the pub.'

'I've only got half an hour you know.'

Margaret had disappeared.

'What do you reckon she says?' Arthur whispered, shoving several chips into his mouth.

'About men.'

'Is that what Elaine says?'

'Yes.'

'She's got a mucky mind, that Elaine.'

'Thank God,' Harry laughed.

The little café was crowded. Behind the counter, Mildred was busy cooking the orders and Elaine was trying to wash up. Margaret was serving on the tables. When Harry and Arthur came in, Elaine waved and blew Harry a kiss, pouting her lips and making a smacking noise everybody in the café heard. She was wearing a white blouse with flare-sleeves and a low neck. Harry noticed how brown she was and wondered when she'd had time to get in the sun. She must have been working on the farm at weekends before the promenade got so busy. Her face was covered with freckles and she was wearing faint pink lipstick.

'Dirty thoughts?' Arthur said, nudging his arm and offering him a cigarette.

'She's always too busy,' Harry frowned. 'Some bloke or other.'

'Can you wonder?'

'She makes me feel stupid.'

'How do you mean?'

'Embarrassed.'

'It's the eyes,' Arthur grinned.

'Is it?'

'Definitely. Go to bed eyes, they are. You can always tell. She's just waiting for me to ask.'

'Shut up. I've got work to do this afternoon.'

'I haven't,' Arthur said happily.

There was an argument going on behind the counter, and when one of the customers shouted out that he was still waiting for his dinner, Elaine grabbed the plate of food and took it across to him. He was on his own and in a hurry. Margaret looked furious. Smiling, Elaine pushed her way between the tables and came and stood next to Harry.

'I could murder a fag,' she said, leaning on their table and massaging her feet.

'Don't you get a break?' Harry asked.

'Not when we're busy. We're always busy, far as I can see.'

She rested her arm on Harry's shoulder and squeezed gently.

'Heard any dirty talk recently?' Arthur grinned innocently.

'You can shut up, 'n' all. I'm in enough trouble already without you joining in.'

'It's all in the imagination,' Arthur said, nodding seriously. 'You hear what you want to hear. It's probably you doing the talking and then thinking it was Margaret. She wouldn't recognise a dirty thought if it was written in the Bible.'

Elaine ignored him, smiling her wide smile at Harry and leaning against his shoulder.

'You going to let me have that free ride, then?' she asked.

'What time do you finish?'

''Bout nine.'

'Come down to Happiland then. I'll be on the floor somewhere.'

'Lovely,' Elaine smirked, raising her eyebrows and glancing across at Mildred who was beginning to look irritated. 'I shall have to go.'

'See you then.'

'See you,' Arthur said cheerfully.

'I hope not.'

'Blimey.' He grinned at Harry appreciatively. 'You're in there, pal.'

'You reckon?'

'Take my word.'

'I wouldn't wait to find out,' Harry shrugged, finishing his meal and getting up ready to go back to Happiland.

'No?'

'No. If she's not a teaser, I'll eat your underwear.'

Shouting to Mildred, they left the café and made their way back along the promenade to Happiland.

The heat that afternoon was scorching, and the fairground remained more or less empty. A few of the regular gamblers stayed all day at the fruit machines, and the housey-housey tables were busy with housewives hoping to win the garish prizes. But Harry had practically nothing to do. He sat on the grand national race and chatted with Les and Clive Smalley. During the breaks, he did a turn on the waltzer and the dodgems, enjoying swinging from car to car and showing off as a couple of girls tried to ram each other on the dodgems. He went on the big dipper with Arthur, and they stood and talked to some of the girls who were playing the records on the juke box. When he went for his tea at five o'clock, he felt fresh and full of energy, and took a quick swim with Arthur as the tide was going out.

'The point is,' Norman was arguing with Clive when they got back to Happiland, 'the point is, it would do you good. Get you fit.'

One of the prostitutes who worked the fairgrounds was sitting with them and she snorted loudly.

'Soldiers I meet ent fit.' She grinned at Norman.

'Shut up.'

'He looks fit enough to me.'

'I am fit,' Clive said.

Norman scoffed.

'You don't look it to me, son. Feel that muscle.'

Clive obliged and squeezed Norman's arm, admiring the bulging muscles.

'Really hard.' He winked at the girl, who cackled loudly.

'And you'd get a trade,' Norman went on. 'I'm trying to explain to this prat the advantages of doing his duty,' he said as Harry and Arthur joined them on the steps of the waltzer.

'I've already got a trade,' Clive said.

'What's that then?'

'Magic.'

Harry and Arthur both laughed but Norman was beginning to look annoyed.

'Don't give me smart answers, lad.'

'It's true. Magic Circle. I'll show you.'

Before Norman could flinch, Clive reached out and took a

half-crown from behind Norman's ear and a silk handkerchief from his shirt pocket.

Norman's eyes bulged, yellow and bruised. His mottled
face went bright red.

'Where did that come from?' he said furiously.

Clive opened his hands and they were empty. His shirt
sleeves were rolled above the elbows. He flicked his hands
over again and a pair of ear-rings lay on the open palms,
cheap gold blinking in the lights of the waltzer.

Coming over to them, Mac stood and watched, smiling
sceptically.

'You could employ this bloke, Mac,' Arthur said. 'He's
wonderful.'

Clive turned his hands again and the ear-rings were gone.

He reached forward and as Norman flinched, he took a
gold sovereign from behind Norman's ear. He held it on the
flat of his palm, and to their amazement, music suddenly
started coming from Clive's hand. Harry glanced up quickly,
thinking he must have something in his mouth, but Clive just
smiled, opening his mouth wide and raising his eyebrows in
mockery.

Norman stood up and hoisted his trousers back up to his
waist.

'Very clever,' he said angrily. 'Impressive and all that. But
will it keep you alive?'

Before Clive could answer, he stalked off, and Mac burst
out laughing, enjoying seeing Norman so annoyed.

'I've not seen him that mad for years,' he said happily.
'Somebody's going to get into trouble tonight.'

The national service lads came down to the fairground at
about eleven o'clock, straight out of the pubs. Ronald Timms
was with them. They were making a lot of noise. Timms was
hard and thin now, his face still unnaturally pale but all the
fat gone, his uniform making him look much older, his eyes
careful and unpleasant.

Harry didn't recognise any of the lads he was with. They

played the fruit machines for a few minutes and shouted and jeered at some of the lasses on the rocket rides, but the Teds had not been back since Sunday, and they didn't know about Clive.

As they were leaving, Timms recognised Harry and came across to him.

'How you keeping, Harry?'

'Not so bad. You look all right.'

'Fit as a fiddle.'

'You look it.'

Ronald grinned, lighting a cigarette and blowing the smoke in Harry's face.

'How's your mate these days?' he asked.

'Arthur?'

'That's the one. All right, is he?'

'Yes, he's around somewhere.'

'Gone on the trawlers, 'as he?'

'No,' Harry shrugged.

'That's good. Be getting your papers soon, Harry?'

'Yes.'

'Great life, it is. I been all over.'

'Yes?'

'Malaya. Aden. Can't beat it. You know these lads?'

The other soldiers had come across and stood watching. Harry nodded to them.

'Old mate of mine,' Ronald explained. 'Just telling him about Malaya. Fucking terrorists. Fucking bastards.'

Two or three of the soldiers laughed, grinning at Harry, waiting to see what he would say.

'Can't stand the black bastards,' one of the soldiers said, winking at Harry.

'Don't have to, do we, lads?'

They all roared with laughter, and Harry saw Timms watching him.

'Got to get on, Ronald,' he said. 'Mac'll be after me. Nice to see you again.'

'End of the year is it, Harry?' Ronald shouted as Harry

walked back towards the office. He glanced over his shoulder and nodded. 'Great life,' Timms repeated, giving the thumbs-up sign. Harry waved and let himself into the office.

For the first time all weekend he felt depressed.

He made a pot of tea and sat in the office with his back to the wall. He could hear the music coming from the juke box room and the shrieks and shouts on the rides. On the grand national race, Les was doing his favourite line of patter, chatting up all the old women, telling them he'd saved the best prizes for them, only the prize was a secret, and he would show them afterwards behind the big dipper. The women loved the way Les went on. He was one of Mac's big attractions.

It was gone midnight by the time the fairground emptied.

Harry and Elaine were sitting together on the steps of the waltzer. She put her arm round his back, and rested her head on his shoulder. Arthur was still playing the fruit machines. In his office, Mac was busy counting the day's takings. Slumped at the housey-housey tables, Norman was slowly draining a bottle of light-ale, oblivious to anything going on around him. Between the golden gallopers and the gypsy fortune-teller, they could see the moon shining on the sea, and the lighthouse at the wide estuary.

'This is nice,' Elaine said, whispering close to his face, her breath warm against his neck.

It was Clive who put the record on.

Earlier in the evening, Mac had brought some new records for the juke box, but nobody had yet had a chance to play them.

In the empty fairground, they could hear the sea washing up the beaches, a drunk singing far away at the other end of the promenade, a police siren wailing its way through the darkness.

'It's nice,' Elaine said again, kissing Harry on the cheek.

When he heard the voice, he felt a shiver go down his back.

He looked up, wondering where it was coming from, not thinking it could be from the records on the juke box. As the guitars went on, he saw Elaine watching him, a slow smile on her face. He heard the guitar wailing, and then the bass thumping, and the piano playing a lazy blues, jabbing at the night silence. When the record ended, nobody said anything, as if they were waiting for somebody to start the juke box again. In Harry's head, the music still echoed, fading as though he had never heard it.

At the fruit machines, Arthur grinned awkwardly.

'What is that?' he said, his hands still on the fruit machine lever, waiting to claim a jackpot.

When Clive came out of the juke box room, he told them it was 'Heartbreak Hotel', by some American called Elvis Presley.

As he shouted goodnight, Harry went and looked at the juke box. He took a handful of coins from his pocket and played the record again. As he listened, Elaine stood at the entrance of the juke box room, and Arthur sat down on one of the benches.

'It's incredible,' Elaine said, smiling at Harry in surprise.

Each time the record began, Harry felt the chill go down his back.

Fourteen

In the weeks before the school holidays the fairgrounds weren't quite so busy and Harry was able to do some bait digging for George Bainbridge, working along the tideline with Herbert Edlin and then sitting in the back yard, baiting the snoods while Jack read the papers or listened to the wireless.

'You don't know what music is,' he scoffed when Harry told him to listen to Fats Domino or Pat Boone.

'Go on then.'

'Charlie Kunz. Whispering Jack Smith.'

'Never heard of them.'

'Hoagy Carmichael.'

'Give over, Jack.'

'Flanagan and Allen. Your mother used to love Flanagan and Allen.'

'I don't believe it,' Harry laughed. 'Dickie Valentine and David Whitfield more like.'

'"Underneath the arches,"' Jack crooned, his face going bright red as he gasped for breath.

When Harry told him to listen to 'Heartbreak Hotel', he lost his temper and thumped the table with his fist, getting so worked up he had a bad coughing fit and had to spend the afternoon resting in bed.

'I had a melodion, you know,' he told Harry one morning when they were sitting in the back yard. 'Used to play down on the quays.'

'How do you mean?'

'The fishergirls, you know. Gutting quines. They used to follow the herring fleets down from Scotland. Lived in wooden huts not far from the docks, six to a room, with a coke stove in the middle of the room. They wore these high leather boots, oilskin skirts and knitted woollen scarves. When they were working, they had cotton rags wrapped round their fingers to protect them from the salt and brine, but they still got deep, painful ulcers. Working out in the yards from six in the morning until it was dark, ankle-deep in mud, sand, and fish refuse. And then on Saturday nights, they'd entertain their friends, singing hymns and dancing on the quays. Sluts, some folk called 'em. Most of them were from Shetland and the Orkneys. You'd see them around town, walking together in groups, laughing and talking and knitting. They all wore these black shawls. I used to go down the quays and play for them. Beautiful it was, that melodion. Hand-carved, with wooden ends decorated with lovely green mermaids. Beautiful little instrument.'

Harry knew Jack was remembering his wife. He sat and listened, and when Jack had finished he went and made some tea. When he came back out into the yard again, Jack had his wallet out.

'Here,' he said, 'you go and get yourself some of them records.'

'I've nowt to play 'em on, Jack.'

'How much do you need then?'

'I'm saving now.'

'No, go on. I've nowt else to do with my money. How much do you need?'

You could get a turntable which plugged into the wireless for twelve pounds ten shillings.

Jack fumbled in his wallet and took out a wad of notes, counting them out into his lap. He put the wallet back in his jacket and handed the notes to Harry.

'There you are,' he said.

'I can't take that, Jack. I'm earning what I need.'

'Take it, I said.'

'Well . . .'

'Only don't expect me to listen to any rubbish. You buy Flanagan and Allen. You buy summat worth listening to. I'm too old for all this modern rubbish.'

*

When he'd finished with the baiting Harry walked up to town to Halfords and bought the turntable. The man in the shop told him to be sure and turn the sound on on the wireless otherwise there'd be nothing to hear. Harry bought 'Heartbreak Hotel' and 'Ain't That a Shame', and then the man handed him a new record that had just come in. It wasn't actually supposed to be released yet, the man said, but Harry could have a copy if he wanted. It was another Elvis Presley, 'Blue Suede Shoes' with 'Tutti Frutti' on the other side. The records came in white cardboard sleeves marked Halfords. They were 2s 3d each, HMV with the blue labels showing a dog staring at a gramophone.

When he got out of the shop, he saw Alison and her stepmother going into Woolworths. He waved to Alison, and she crossed the road to see what he'd bought. She was wearing a yellow dress with a flared skirt and sharply pointed shoes. She looked happy and cheerful as though she was glad to be out of the house and not studying.

'What's that, Harry?'

'Record player.'

Peering into the bag, she took the records out and looked at the labels.

'You want to listen?' Harry said, watching her.

Her hair hid her eyes, and when she looked up she was smiling, her face pale in the sunlight.

She bit her lip.

'I'm supposed to be shopping,' she said.

'Please yourself.'

'Is your mother at home?'

'Don't be daft, Alison.'

Nervously, she glanced over towards the shops and then touched Harry's arm, giggling and brushing her hair out of her eyes.

They walked down the road past the cinema and the railway station and across the waste land to fishermen's lanes. When they got to the house, Harry's mother was in the kitchen getting dinner, and Alison stood in the doorway, chatting to her about school and exams. Harry went through to the front room and plugged the turntable into the wireless they kept in there. He could hear his mother asking about Dr Milburn, and then she shouted through to see if he wanted a cup of tea.

'No thanks,' he said, taking one of the records out of its cardboard sleeve.

He could hear his mother laughing about the turntable, saying that her father had been throwing his money about again.

Harry turned the volume up and started the record.

After hearing 'Heartbreak Hotel' so many times, the new record was a shock. He jumped up the minute it started and turned the volume down, then turned it back up again. He played 'Blue Suede Shoes' first, and then 'Tutti Frutti'. When 'Blue Suede Shoes' finished for the second time he heard Jack banging on the bedroom floor with his boot and turned round to find his mother standing in the doorway, holding her hands to her ears.

'What on earth's that?' she said, Alison standing right behind her giggling.

Harry went to put the record on again but his mother raised her hand, going to close the door.

'No, please. Let me get out.'

Alison grinned, shaking her head.

'He's no taste, Mrs Kelam,' she was saying as the door closed.

Harry turned the record on again and stared at it as it spun round. With the volume right up, he didn't hear his grandfather, or Mrs Blakey next door, rattling her poker at the back of the grate. In the street, people going past glanced towards the sitting-room window. He sat and listened to 'Blue Suede Shoes', and wondered how anybody could make such a wonderful sound, the slapping bass, the guitars twanging and echoing, the wailing voice, yelling into the small front room. He felt his pulse beginning to race, and he wanted to jump up and do something to the music, clap or dance round the room, get hold of somebody and shout. He sat, amazed at what he was hearing. He couldn't believe his mother and Alison would stay in the kitchen, not wanting to listen to what he had bought. He put the record on for the fourth time when his mother came through and told him angrily to play something else.

'It's not my kind of music, that's all,' Alison complained when he kept going on at her about her not liking the records.

They were walking back along the promenade, hurrying because Alison was late for lunch. When they reached the Winter Gardens, she stood with him waiting for his tram. He had to get back to work.

'You must be deaf,' he said angrily, staring at the ornamental gardens.

'So must you, the way you had the sound turned up,' she said sarcastically.

'You have to have it turned up.'

'Your mother didn't like it.'

'She's old.'

'Don't be stupid, Harry.'

'She is.'

He felt angry, resentful. He wanted her to like the records, see why he found them exciting.

She had just laughed with his mother, refusing to listen.

'You can't hear the words,' his mother mocked when he told her what was on the records.

'Yes you can.'

'Tutti Frutti! They're not words.'

'I thought you couldn't hear them?'

'Be bop a wam bam,' Alison giggled.

They'd stood together in the kitchen, giggling and fooling about, laughing at him and pretending to be worried about Mrs Blakey next door.

'She might call the police,' Harry's mother said seriously,

and they had both sat at the kitchen table, giggling like young schoolgirls.

'There's your tram,' Alison said gently, trying to take his arm.

'Sod off, Alison.'

'Don't be like that.'

He could see there were tears in her eyes.

'Sod off.'

'I'm late for my lunch, Harry. I'll be in enough trouble as it is, you know what she's like.'

'So?'

When the tram came, he got on without saying a word. He sat on one of the sideseats by the window, and when he'd got his ticket, turned to look back. Alison was walking away from the Winter Gardens. When she turned to go down her street, he waved, but she didn't see him. He sat slumped on his seat, furious at their ridicule, miserable and disappointed.

Fifteen

Keith was in Mildred's early one Friday morning.

A white mist lay across the river. At the estuary, the warning bell was ringing on the buoy. The pier floated eerily above the fog, its green roof shining in the watery sunlight.

Harry had been out digging since dawn, and he sat down at Keith's table and waited for Elaine to bring them a pot of tea. He hadn't seen Keith for weeks. His face was white, hollowed, and the skin beneath his eyes was bruised and swollen. His hair was cropped to the bone, and he looked as though he had been close-shaving several times a day, his cheeks mottled and blotched with dried blood.

Elaine brought them their tea and then went back to her seat behind the counter, polishing her fingernails and listening to the two of them talk. When Harry came into the café, she looked at him absent-mindedly and smiled. Bringing the tea, she touched his shoulder lightly, avoiding his eyes when he looked up.

'My mum's more upset,' Keith was saying.

His hand shook as he lifted his cup, and when he tried to drink, a trickle of hot tea ran down the side of his mouth. He wiped it away angrily and stared out of the window.

'Sorry.'

'Don't be daft.'

On the promenade, a dog emerged briefly out of the fog, and then disappeared down the wide steps to the sands. Along the green railings, hundreds of seagulls perched, waiting for the fog to lift.

'They get us doing such stupid things,' Keith said, his eyes filling with tears.

'What kind of things?'

'Shaving the handles of sweeping brushes, so they're just white wood. That kind of thing.'

'I don't believe you.'

'I had to do that.'

'Why?'

'And they stand right in front of you,' Keith said. 'Screaming abuse. Right close to your face. You can't move. Spitting in your face.'

Behind the counter, Elaine finished polishing her nails and got a bottle of nail polish from her handbag. As she worked, frowning in concentration, she bit her tongue, leaning forward on her chair to hold the brush steady.

'I've got this sergeant,' Keith said, 'called Watters. He's always going on about what we do in bed. Sneering. Sniggering. He . . . He . . .'

Harry looked away.

After a moment, Keith blew his nose and rubbed his jacket sleeve across his face. He was wearing his ordinary clothes. Most of the lads coming back from Catterick wore their uniforms everywhere they went, showing off.

'I'm going to see Winifred Atwell,' Keith said suddenly, glaring at Harry. 'My parents got special tickets. We're staying in a hotel.'

'In London?'

'Yes.'

'Better than Florence Eliot,' Harry laughed.

Florence Eliot was a piano player who visited the pier every year. Her season was due to start any week.

They paid for the tea and walked along the promenade to Happiland.

Mac was already there, unwinding the green shutters.

Keith sat in the juke box room, listening to the new records. He said he couldn't stop long. Harry knew he was going to clear out before any of the other lads from Catterick came down to the fairgrounds and saw him without his uniform.

'I like something with a tune,' he told Harry when the records finished. 'Something you can sing.'

'My dad's the one I can't stand,' Elaine said, sitting with him at the housey-housey game. 'Always going on. He thinks he owns me.'

At the back of the fairground, Norman and several of the men were struggling with one of the cars on the ghost train, trying to lift it off its track. Four or five drunken fishermen had got out of the car half-way through the tunnel, and the wheels had been twisted and then jammed into the metal rails.

Mac stood on the platform of the ghost train, shouting instructions down the tunnel, wiping the top of his head with his handkerchief. He said he was too claustrophobic to go inside the tunnel and help.

'You don't live there now,' Harry said vaguely.

He'd seen Clive go off with the girl who ran the rifle range. She was new on the fairground that year. Mac said she'd been thrown out of the high school for breaking a chair over a teacher's head, but when he asked Alison about her she didn't know her name.

'They still expect me to visit,' Elaine sighed.

She was wearing one of the new hooped skirts, the flared orange material bright and garish against her black jumper, huge gold ear-rings dangling from her ears. Her fingernails were painted black, and on her cheeks she had thick orange panstick.

'Listen to sermons.'

Harry laughed.

He couldn't imagine Elaine listening to anybody.

'You don't know my parents,' she shrugged, smiling at him.

As she spoke, she touched his arm, stroking the inside of his elbow. He looked away across the fairground to where Mac was arguing with Les, telling him he didn't know what

96

he was talking about. It sounded as though the ghost train was going to take some sorting.

Getting up from the housey-housey tables, Harry slipped a coin into the fortune telling machine and waited until the gypsy had decided on his future. When the printed card emerged, it said that he was going on a long journey and that he would be lucky in love. He flipped the card to Elaine and wandered across to the juke box room.

Elaine followed him.

He used his keys to free the selector and punched in 'Only You' and 'Heartbreak Hotel'. He didn't feel in the mood for anything noisy. He sat down on one of the wooden benches and closed his eyes. Elaine moved next to him. When the two records finished, they sat together without speaking, the sound of laughter drifting down the fairground from the ghost train, the hum of a generator steady in the warm silence.

Ever since he'd seen Keith he'd been feeling restless, unable to settle down or concentrate on his work. He kept thinking about how they used to meet on the pier, sitting in the wooden shelter at the end with Arthur and Joanne Mottram, telling stupid jokes and smoking cigarettes. Joanne had two children now. Soon, Arthur would be getting his papers.

Elaine took his hand and squeezed it.

'Come on,' she said firmly.

'Where?'

'Anywhere. Down the prom.'

They walked out of the fairground and along the promenade towards the pier. The illuminations had been turned off and the promenade was deserted, only Happiland still showing a light. Elaine wouldn't let go of his hand. When they reached the pier, she stopped by the ticket office and pulled his arm round her shoulders.

'You going to show me?' she said, her face close up to him, her breath warm on his cheeks.

'What?'

'The end of the pier. Arthur told me.'

'You've already been.'

'Not in the summer.'

'All right.'

The gates were locked. He had to help her climb over. When she jumped down, she caught his hand to balance, and they stood together at the entrance, listening to the surf crashing up the deserted shores, the dark sea washing against the groynes.

Harry suddenly felt tired.

He let Elaine take his hand and lead the way out to the end of the pier. In the wooden shelter, they sat down and started to kiss. Over her shoulder, he saw the sky packed with stars, brilliant with moonlight. Down on the docks, the red light shone on the dock tower.

Elaine sat back and brushed the hair out of her eyes.

'Don't you like me?' she said, and he stared at her, confused, wanting to hide his face. 'Don't you?'

'Don't be stupid.'

'Well then?'

He leaned forward and rested his head on her shoulders.

Elaine stroked the back of his neck, her breath warm on his face, her hands gentle and making him feel sleepy.

Yawning, she got some of his hair in her mouth and sneezed loudly, the noise echoing down the pier. On the roof, a dozen seagulls clamoured in panic, wheeling into the dark and screaming away over the sea.

'They think it's Arthur with his calcium carbonate,' Harry joked, and helpless with laughter, Elaine lay in his arms, tears running down her cheeks and wetting his face and neck.

When she stopped laughing, she lay perfectly still in his arms, and he kissed her on the side of her nose, licking the tears and making her giggle. Moving closer, she unfastened her ear-rings and put them down on the bench.

'That's better,' she whispered as he kissed her on the mouth.

He could feel her breasts through the black jumper. As she

loosened the belt on her skirt he pushed his hands inside and touched the bare skin, the firm nipples. Elaine groaned quickly, squirming against him.

'Have you got anything?' she said, biting the side of his face.

'What?'

Harry sat back but she held him close, saying it didn't matter. He wanted to go, get up and leave the pier, but she started unfastening his trousers and when her hands started stroking him between the legs he suddenly clung to her desperately, hurting her shoulder and digging his hands into her bare skin underneath the jumper.

'You're going to have to lie down,' she giggled, kissing the side of his face lightly with the end of her tongue.

'Yes.'

'I'm not ruining this skirt.'

The boards were hard underneath his back. He could hear the sea, rumbling in the darkness. Far away, a railway engine was shunting trucks in the yards.

Kneeling down, Elaine lifted her skirt and put his hand between her legs. He closed his eyes. She was wet and her legs were warm, hot between the thighs. He could hardly breathe. She pulled his trousers down and the splintered boards made him gasp, rough and cold on his skin. Elaine giggled. She sat over him, and started to stroke him. As her fingers touched him, he opened his eyes and stared at her in panic. 'Don't,' he started to say, but she was already trying to press him between her legs, still holding his cock as he cried out and held himself rigid against the floor. 'Don't.' He felt his come soaking her hand, and she gave a quick gasp of shock, and then squeezed hard as he shouted out in the darkness, squeezing him until he lay still and the cold wetness ran down his legs, her fingers still holding him and her eyes closed when he finally looked at her.

'Fool,' she said when she saw that he was crying. 'Stupid bloody fool.'

In the dark, she lay down on top of him, and soon he could hear her quiet breathing as she slept.

When they woke up, she lit a cigarette.

'What time is it?' she asked.

Harry could hardly move.

He peered at his watch.

'Two o'clock.'

'Already.'

'It was gone one when we left,' he said quietly.

He felt awkward, sitting on the wooden boards.

He didn't want to speak.

As she smoked, he watched the light at the far end of the promenade where they were still working in Happiland.

'They'll never finish that ghost train,' he said.

'Not without you.'

'One of our most popular rides.'

'You'll have to go back and help,' Elaine smiled, touching his lips very lightly with the tips of her fingers.

She finished the cigarette and they sat together without speaking.

'What are you thinking about?' she said.

'Keith,' he said after a pause.

'Not that Alison?'

'No.'

'You must be queer,' she giggled. 'I don't think about women.'

'He's a mate,' Harry said, struggling into his trousers and taking hold of her hand. 'Ever since I can remember.'

Elaine shivered and snuggled in his arms.

'I'm cold.'

'Yes.'

'You walk us back, Harry?'

'Yes.'

He stood up and leaned on the railings. A long way away, several miles beyond the estuary, he could see the lights of a trawler, steaming towards the coast. It would be hurrying for the morning market, racing to catch the lumpers before they finished unloading. In the heat, the catch might go off if the trawler had to stay offshore all day.

'Don't be upset, Harry,' Elaine whispered, getting up and leaning on his arm.

'I'm not.'

'Yes you are.'

In her arms, he buried his head against her shoulder and suddenly began to cry. He felt tired, exhausted. As he wept, she rocked him in her arms and kept up a low moaning sound. She kept telling him it was all right, nothing was the matter.

Far away, a ship's siren wailed, acknowledging the green light on the lockpit.

Sixteen

It was incredibly hot.

In the middle of the night, Harry got out of bed and walked across town. He thought about Elaine. She was visiting her parents on the farm where her father worked. Any day now they would begin the first harvest. The peas would soon be cropped, and the air would be thick with small black flies. They got into your hair and under your clothes, inflaming the skin if you scratched them. He wondered if Elaine was asleep, what time she would be getting back tomorrow.

'I'll see you at Mildred's,' she said as she was leaving.

'When?'

'When I get back, fool.'

He watched her bus drive out of the bus station and went and had a drink in the transport café, not wanting to leave the station.

'You're going soft,' Mildred said crossly when he sat in the café early the following morning, staring out of the windows. 'She's only gone for two days.'

Still, Harry couldn't sleep.

He walked through town without thinking where he was going.

Outside the church in the main street, a drunk was sleeping in the graveyard. He lay flat on his back, his mouth open, his arms thrown wide apart. In the silence, Harry stood and listened to the drunken snoring, and the steady hum of the dimmed streetlights.

A long way off, he heard a car door slam, and a minute later a car turned into the street and went past very fast. It was a woman driving. As Harry stood outside the church, she turned and glanced at him, pushing her hand back through her hair. She seemed surprised, lifting her hand in a brief greeting and then looking away quickly. He heard the car engine for a long time, fading through the empty streets.

When he reached his old secondary school, he stood for some minutes at the gates, staring round the big playground. It was still divided into two by the railing, but the benches had been removed. Perhaps somebody had complained. He jumped over the low wall and walked round the playground in a circle, following the white lines that had been painted out for games.

He'd hated the school.

The English teacher was a fat, elderly man called Smith. He had been teaching in the school for years and was due for retirement. He told Harry's class one afternoon that they were going to read *The Wind in the Willows*. Harry had a copy of the book at home. His grandfather had bought it for him at a bazaar at the Seamen's Mission. They read it together, sitting by the fire, listening to the wind rattle the kitchen windows, the rain lash down the chimney.

When Smith asked one of the boys to hand the books out, Harry put his hand up.

'I've read that, sir,' he told the teacher, leaning back in his chair and ignoring the sniggers that went round the class.

The teacher was furious.

His round, fat face went bright red and he glared at Harry through his silver-framed glasses.

'You're too stupid to read a book like this, Kelam,' he shouted, and everybody in the class roared with laughter.

Harry blushed.

They had to read the book out loud, and when the reading got round to him, he refused to speak. Smith sent him to the headmaster for the cane, but he just wandered out of the school and down the promenade. Arthur saw him from the classroom window as he was leaving the playground and got up and followed him.

They both got the cane the following morning.

Going up on to the verandah, Harry stood outside one of

the classrooms and stared into the room, the neat rows of desks and clean blackboard, the high teacher's desk. He walked the length of the verandah until he reached the metalwork rooms. Everybody in the school had to do woodwork and metalwork. It was part of their preparation for jobs. The metalwork teacher had been in the RAF during the war, and he threw lumps of metal around when he lost his temper, raging at spoiled work. In the woodwork classes, Harry got the cane nearly every week during his first term, and then smashed a towel rail on the edge of an open door, splintering the wood and ramming the broken ends into the blade of the lathe. After that, the woodwork teacher left him alone.

It was during their final year at the school that they had all the visits from employment officers.

After the sinking of the *Lincoln Castle* and the *Countess* with the loss of forty lives, the industry had been short of apprentices, and the school had several visits from overweight middle-aged men going on about what a wonderful career the fishing was.

One particular man called Morton came three times.

Harry remembered his face, round and unusually white, the skin tight under his eyes. He'd talked rapidly, wheezing as though repeating a speech made several times before. When he laughed, the fat at his neck wobbled but his eyes didn't change expression. Mostly, he stared out of the window, or down at his notes. Nobody in the class was very interested in what he had to say.

'You can always work on the docks, of course,' he'd joked, dismissing the idea with a quick smile. 'But if you want real money and haven't got the necessary qualifications for an apprenticeship, you have to earn it, don't you? Don't get anything for free in this world.'

'That why you went to sea then?' Arthur interrupted, yawning insolently and resting his feet on his desk.

In the corner, the form teacher, Taplin, looked up, glowering around the classroom. He was marking some papers. His spectacles were heavily rimmed and the glass was thick, distorting his eyes. When he smiled, everybody in the class-room went quiet. He stared at Arthur, not speaking. Earlier that year, Arthur had been put on probation for stealing a bike from outside a shop. The idea had been a bet, Arthur having his right ankle in a bandage after a fall helping with the boats at the slipway. Taplin stared around the room silently, his eyes invisible behind the thick glass. When everybody was quiet he went back to his marking. The man from the employment exchange fidgeted the papers in front of him.

'My dad was drowned at sea,' Harry told him when they each had a personal interview. The man nodded but did not look up from the papers he was reading. Harry stared out of the window to the playing fields where a class was exercising, the gym teacher jumping up and down in front of them and shouting something about ignorant louts.

'Don't you have anything else?' Harry asked when the man didn't look up.

'Anything else?'

'I'm not going on the trawlers.'

'Nobody's forcing you, son. I'm looking through the vacancies if you can just hold your water for a minute.'

His father had been lost in 1951, off Bear Island. One of the neighbours came in afterwards and made a pot of tea. Harry could only remember that the tea was too strong. His mother liked her tea hot and weak.

'It's difficult, you see,' the man said, still not looking up.

He frowned and then sat back in his chair, putting his hands behind his head. His hair was greasy and very black, a lump of Brylcreem on the collar of his jacket.

'The trouble is, you don't have anything to offer,' the man said. 'Labouring is about all there is.'

'That's all right.'

'Not very good money.'

He gave him a card with the name of a building company on the docks.

'Send the next lad in,' he said.

When Harry got outside, he tore the card up and dropped it into a bin.

An owl cried somewhere over the playing fields.

Standing on the verandah, Harry listened.

Nothing stirred.

'Fucking dump,' he said to himself, leaning against the windows of one of the rooms.

He took his clasp knife out of his pocket and carved a big 'FUCK' on the door that led into the headmaster's office.

At the gates, he broke the 'Please Keep Closed' sign off the gate and walked casually away, leaving the gate wide open.

As he sauntered up the deserted street, he felt ridiculous.

Nothing moved on the foreshore.

The moon was like an arc-lamp over the sea, brilliant in the immense sky. Millions of stars stretched from the coast to the horizon. On Sanctuary Point, he could see the black and white of the lighthouse quite clearly, standing out on the jut of land.

He found some shells and skimmed them hard over the flat surface of the water.

They spun and skittered in the moonlight, and then disappeared.

By one of the groynes, he picked up a great mass of seaweed, wet and stinking in the warm night, clinging to the rotting wood. He carried the seaweed right to the edge of the water, and stood with his plimsolls still on in the sea, heaving the seaweed up into the air and flinging it as far out as he could manage. It fell with a light splash, and spread out in great circles in the low waves, washing back slowly into the coal and oil at the filthy strandline.

Running along the edge of the water, he gathered fresh armfuls of the weed, bending down and heaping it into his arms, lifting it and hurling it with all his strength. Each time it splashed into the waves and fanned steadily back to shore, washing around his feet.

As he worked his way along the tideline, more and more of the foul weed flooded back to the spot where he was standing, drifting in huge lumps on the shallow, warm tide.

Laughing, he turned and walked home, the clock at the railway station saying half-past four.

His mother was sitting in the kitchen.

'You want some tea, pet?' she smiled. 'Kettle's boiled.'

She was still wearing her dressing-gown, her feet resting on a chair in the doorway, her hair tied back behind her ears. He got a cup from the cupboard and poured himself a cup of tea. He drew a chair up beside her and stirred sugar into his tea.

'Can't you sleep?' she smiled.

'No. Bit restless.'

'It's the heat,' she said.

They sat together without speaking.

Over the houses, the first faint light of morning was beginning to climb out of the sea. On the foreshore, the gulls were starting their racket. Harry wondered whether Herbert would be out digging.

'Your dad used to like this time,' his mother said. 'Before things got started, he used to say. We often came and sat down here when he was home from a trip.'

'I didn't know that.'

His mother laughed.

'You weren't walking the streets every hour God sends in those days,' she said.

'Sorry.'

'I don't mind, love. Long as you don't get hurt.'

'I won't get hurt, Mum.'

'No, I know, pet.'

'She's all right.'

'Is she?'

'Yes.'

'What about Alison?'

Harry shrugged, staring at his hands.

'She'll be gone soon,' he said.

'Not for ever.'

'Maybe.'

'Not Alison.'

He finished his tea and washed the cup at the sink.

'Did my dad do national service?' he asked suddenly.

He never talked about his father. Never asked questions.

His mother shook her head.

'He was on the minesweepers,' she said. 'Most fishermen did that. He wouldn't have liked anything else.'

'Not the army?'

'No.'

'I'm not going in the army,' he said.

He could feel his eyes filling with tears.

'I'm sorry.'

'You're just tired, pet.'

'I know.'

'Something'll come up.'

'I'm not going on the trawlers either,' Harry said suddenly. 'I'm not going to sea like Dad.'

The tears were pouring down his face.

His mother stood up, pulling him into her arms.

'Harry,' she said, alarmed. She looked into his face, her eyes quick and concerned. 'What on earth's the matter?'

'I'm not going on the trawlers, that's all.'

'But of course you're not. Whoever said you should?'

'Or the army.'

'Bugger the army,' his mother laughed, holding him tightly in her arms. 'Bugger the sodding army.'

Laughing, he dried his face.

'Yes,' he said, grinning at her and wiping his eyes. 'Bugger the sodding army.'

Out in the passage, the milkman was rattling his crates, whistling as he came round to the backs.

'You'll do nothing you don't want to,' Harry's mother told him seriously. 'Do you hear me?'

'Yes, course.'

'Nothing you don't want to.'

As the milkman crashed open the yard gate, Harry suddenly felt as though none of it mattered. He could do what he wanted. Like working for Mac on Happiland, or bait digging for George Bainbridge. He would have to find a way. Like Clive, and all the other lads.

Rubbing his eyes, he told his mother about Elaine.

He said she had been away, visiting her parents, in a village a few miles out of town.

She would be waiting for him now at Mildred's, ready with a cooked breakfast and a pot of fresh tea.

'She makes a lovely cup of tea,' he told her, and laughed when she pulled a face.

'She does,' he said, clearing the things off the table.

His mother just laughed.

'You'll never persuade your grand-dad,' she said as she got ready to do the breakfast.

When he went upstairs to wash and get some different clothes, he could hear his mother in the kitchen, laying the table and boiling another kettle. She had to be at the laundry by half past eight, and Jack would soon be down demanding his bacon and eggs. By the time Harry had dressed, Jack was already coughing, and he ran back down the stairs and gave his mother a quick kiss, shouting goodbye as he ran up the passage.

Seventeen

Mac filled the juke box with rock 'n' roll.

The charts were still full of records by Winifred Atwell and Teresa Brewer, David Whitfield and Kay Starr, and crowds queued every night to see Florence Eliot on the pier where she had begun her new season of concerts, but in the juke box room all they wanted to hear was the new music.

'Give the people what they want,' Mac told Harry when each new delivery of records arrived. 'It's not my money they're wasting.'

'They should be so lucky,' Les jeered.

Mac preferred Geraldo.

'Ted Heath and his Music at the Gaiety,' he said.

'Who?'

'You've no taste, boy.'

'I've never heard of 'em.'

Some nights when the fairground wasn't too busy, Mac went dancing at the Café Dansant. His date was a big secret.

'An affair written on the wind,' Norman explained mysteriously.

'What's that mean, Norman?' Harry asked.

'Ahh,' said Norman with a self-satisfied smile. 'If you but knew, if you but knew.'

Harry got on with his work and didn't worry about what Mac was doing.

He had not seen Alison since their argument about his records. He knew she was busy with her exams, the ones that would get her into university, and the night she came down to the fairground to see him, he was with Elaine, having a drink at the Dolphin.

Elaine he saw nearly every night.

She came along to Happiland as soon as Mildred's had

110

closed. If he was busy, she would sit in the juke box room, listening to the latest records. When he took his breaks, they would go for walks along the sands, stand and watch the sea. At the end of the day, while Mac was checking the cash, she would sit with him on the waltzer and argue with Norman about India, telling him he didn't know what he was talking about. When Harry asked her why she knew so much about the country, she said she didn't, she'd made it all up. Once the fairground was closed, he would walk her home back to Mildred's.

'I'm not going to stay,' she said one night when she'd had a big row with Margaret.

She complained bitterly about having to share a bedroom.

'But you've got to sleep somewhere,' Harry pointed out.

'I shall sleep at the café.'

'Don't be daft, Elaine.'

'There's room at the back.'

'But you can't sleep there . . .'

She ignored him, scuffing her shoes along the edge of the pavement. The previous owner of the café had slept in the back room on a camp bed, and Elaine had found out, but Harry couldn't see Mildred ever agreeing.

'She says she's concerned about my moral welfare,' Elaine scoffed.

'There isn't a bed, more likely,' Harry grinned.

'So?'

'You'd have to sleep on the floor. All them rats.'

'Don't be stupid.'

'Huge, they are.'

'Try telling Mildred that.'

One night when they arrived at Mildred's house, she took his hand and led him into the shadows in the garden. Whispering, she told him they were underneath her bedroom, the bedroom she shared with Margaret. Harry glanced up and she started giggling, leaning back against the wall. He felt her face warm against his own, and when they were kissing she kept her mouth open, her lips warm and soft, her tongue exploring his mouth. He felt dizzy with exhaustion, his stomach churning, his heartbeat pulsing in his ears. He felt her hands unfastening his trousers, and as he felt inside her jumper and pulled it over her head, she made him turn round so that his back was against the wall, and lifted her skirt to press herself against him. He was hard and excited, feeling her breasts in his hands, and as he pushed inside her she had to keep a hand over his mouth, stopping him from shouting out and then giggling herself as he writhed back into the wall, gasping for breath and grazing his shoulder as he slipped, falling clumsily so that they both ended up on the lawn.

As he closed his eyes, he saw a light go on in the bedroom, and Elaine hushed him to be quiet. He thought Margaret was going to open the window, but Elaine said she always slept with it shut.

'She thinks she'll lose her soul with it open,' she whispered, giggling close to his ear.

'Liar.'

'She does,' Elaine insisted. 'I promise you.'

On the wet grass, she slowly roused him again, and when he was ready she sat across him, leaning forward so that he could kiss her breasts, reaching behind her and teasing him with one hand.

As they came, a cat stalked across the lawn, but neither of them saw it.

Each night, when Harry got home, he lay awake for hours, thinking about the things Elaine had said, the way she felt in his arms. Some mornings he was still awake when a pink light filled his bedroom and he heard the gulls and terns at the tideline, the steady fall of the sea up the shores. He got out of bed early and went for walks along the promenade, waiting for Mildred's to open, and Elaine to start serving breakfast. His mother said she never saw him. One morning he stood at the café windows and blew kisses to Elaine through the glass, blushing when Mildred saw him and waved him to come in. While Mildred went into the back to open some fresh coffee, he sat at a table waiting for his cup of tea. When Elaine brought it, she touched his hand, and bent down to kiss him on the mouth. She smelt of grass and toothpaste, fresh as spring dew, her mouth warm from a cup of tea.

Some mornings he got up extra early and went down to the tideline, walking miles along the deserted shores, his wellingtons splashing through the shallow water, the morning sunlight climbing slowly out of the sea. Herbert was usually digging, getting bait for the pleasure fishermen or an occasional special order for the inshore fishermen. Harry would stand and watch while Herbert worked, and ask him questions about his grandfather. When Herbert finished, they would go up to Brown's and eat an enormous breakfast, joking about the prices tourists would pay for the worms, the daft advice Herbert gave to visitors when they asked him the best spots to do some line-fishing.

One night, when Elaine was waiting on the waltzer, Mac offered her a job.

'I'll pay you more than Mildred,' he promised her, but she just laughed, refusing to answer.

'I don't see how you can refuse,' Mac said with a puzzled frown. 'Nobody refuses money.'

'I like doing what I want,' Elaine said mischievously.

Mac shrugged and walked away.

'You must be mad,' Harry told her. 'I wish I could afford to turn down money.'

'I like Mildred,' Elaine lied blatantly.

When he laughed, she refused to talk to him.

On a Thursday, towards the end of the month, she visited the fairground one evening when Harry was still busy, helping Mac empty the fruit machines. Harry saw her sitting at the housey-housey, talking to Clive Smalley. By the time he had finished with Mac, Elaine had gone. Clive was nowhere to be seen.

'Went for a walk,' Norman said bleakly when Harry asked him if he'd seen them leave.

The next day, Elaine wasn't at work. She'd gone to visit her parents, Mildred told him irritably, and he remembered her warning him about the visit.

Clive cheerfully avoided him all day.

'You're imagining it,' Arthur said, sitting with him in Brown's on the Saturday morning.

Harry had been bait digging, a special order for George Bainbridge that Herbert couldn't manage to fill.

His hands were blistered and bruised with hurrying.

Arthur wasn't working.

He hadn't seen Elaine for two days.

'She's not like that,' Arthur insisted.

'No?'

'I'm telling you.'

'They're all like that.'

'Don't be stupid.'

'Oh, shut up, Arthur.'

He felt sorry as soon as he'd said it. He could see Arthur was upset.

It was Arthur who had seen them in town, coming out of one of the pubs near the town centre.

'They probably just met,' Arthur said lamely.

'Sure.'

'Just having a drink.'

Harry sighed and slumped in his seat.

He was tired and irritable, and didn't feel like talking.

'It doesn't matter,' he said, trying to sound as though he didn't care.

Arthur didn't look at him.

Later in the week, he had a big row with his grandfather.

He'd woken him up, coming in late from Happiland, and in the morning, Jack was furious.

'Your mother has to go to work, you know.'

'I didn't wake her up.'

'She can't be doing without her sleep.'

'I know, all right!'

'If you got yourself a decent job . . .'

'I have,' Harry shouted, crashing a plate into the sink and smashing it to pieces.

His grandfather bunched his fist and pushed it in Harry's face.

'Twenty years ago, I'd have thumped you for that,' he snarled, his face white with anger, his faded eyes shining with a strange fury.

Harry slammed out of the kitchen, nearly taking the door off its hinges, and went for a long walk beyond the boating lake and the Fitties where they had seen the dead man in the tree on the day after the floods. He walked without thinking where he was going, his hands shaking, his face flushed with temper. Crossing the road near the Winter Gardens, he was nearly run over by a car and yelled abuse after the driver, waving his fists and running several yards down the road before realising how stupid he looked. Out on the coast road, he felt the salt wind on his face and suddenly felt cold, though the sun was high in the sky and the wind was warm. By the time he reached the farm where they had seen the police and army vehicles, he had almost forgotten. He looked up, surprised to see where he was. He stood, staring out over the foreshores, wondering what he was doing.

On Saturday night, Elaine met him outside Happiland.

'My mother was ill,' she explained when he asked her where she'd been. 'She had a stomach upset. I had to stay and help.'

They walked in silence, Harry refusing to hold her hand.

'I thought you'd gone,' he said when she brushed against his arm.

'Gone?'

'I thought you'd left.'

She stopped and turned to look at him.

'I've been at home, helping with my mother.'

'Yes.'

'I haven't seen anybody.'

He felt stupid, standing in the road.

'I'm sorry,' he said.

'Yes.'

'I thought you were seeing somebody.'

'Oh Harry . . .'

'I thought . . .'

'Stop.'

She held him tightly in her arms, caressing the back of his neck.

'This is a daft way to waste our time,' she said.

'I'm sorry.'

'I thought you would have missed me.'

They stood together as a car went past, blinded by the full headlights.

'We'll go on the pier,' Elaine whispered.

Leaning on his arm, she let Harry lead the way.

Eighteen

He took several mornings off to mend some lines for George Bainbridge. In the narrow yard, his grandfather sat and read the newspaper. It was airless and humid. Jack couldn't stand the heat. His face was mottled and bright red in the scorching sunlight, and his breath whistled through his teeth. If he worked himself up into a temper, his face convulsed into a choking cough, and he spat long strings of phlegm into the drain.

'That Florence Eliot's back,' he said one morning, squinting at the newspaper.

'Yes.'

'Bloody tart. She was a beauty queen or summat, before the war. Lot of fancy nonsense.'

Harry listened to his grandfather without much interest. SEE FLORENCE ELIOT all the bunting along the promenade announced, and a large photograph outside the pier showed the star smiling, surrounded by silver candelabra and men in red tuxedos. Miss Eliot gave a concert every evening with jugglers and a well-known magician, and ran a talent competition in the afternoons to encourage local musicians. She even managed to do a show on Sundays, playing religious music and getting the audience to join in, and in the mornings, she gave free demonstrations for charity. But her real claim to fame was that she had played the piano non-stop for longer than anybody else, and this season would be trying to beat her own record.

'Bloody tart,' Jack said again suddenly, screwing the paper up and dropping it beside his chair. 'She must be fifty.'

'Doesn't make her a tart.'

'She broke men's hearts,' Jack said, glaring round the yard.

Harry laughed, glancing at his grandfather.

'She break your heart then, Jack? She give you a good chase for your money?'

His grandfather said nothing, staring out of the gate to the passage between the backs of the houses. He was a miserable sod when he got into one of his tempers, and wouldn't answer unless he felt like it. He took a long drink from the glass of beer beside his chair and wiped the back of his neck with a grimy handkerchief.

'She nearly killed one bloke,' he said eventually, when Harry kept pestering. 'When they got divorced, he was a broken man. It was in all the papers.'

Harry heard the footsteps coming up the passage and dropped the line he was working on.

He thought it was going to be Elaine, and when Alison walked into the yard, he stared at her in surprise, making her laugh at his blank expression.

'It hasn't been that long,' she laughed, nodding to Harry's grandfather. 'How are you keeping, Mr Ellis?'

'I'm fine, lass, fine. Just trying to talk sense to this bugger.'

Harry fetched a chair from the kitchen, and went back to mending the lines.

'Are your exams finished?' he said as Alison watched him working.

'Last week.'

'You look tired.'

She had had her dark hair cut short and square at the neck, and her eyes shone nearly black against her pale skin.

'I'm recovering,' she smiled.

'Jack was just telling me about Florence Eliot,' Harry explained. 'How she once broke his heart.'

'Oh yes,' Alison giggled.

'Take no notice,' Jack grunted. 'He's all blether.'

'I think she's lovely,' Alison said.

'That's right, pet.'

'You lying old bugger,' Harry said.

'Did you know she was playing all night?' Alison said.

'Is that right?'

'I think it's wonderful.'

Harry scoffed.

'She's a fraud,' he said briefly, concentrating on the lines. 'Anybody can see that.'

When Jack went to make some tea, Alison asked him if he wanted to go to the cinema.

'It's *Blackboard Jungle*,' she said. 'The one we went to see last year.'

Harry shifted in his chair uncomfortably.

He remembered the film. A gang from Hull had smashed every seat in the cinema and danced up and down the aisles, throwing darts at the usherettes. Alison's stepmother said they were all yobs and told Alison she was not to go again.

'We'll be all right if we're upstairs,' she giggled, thanking Jack when he brought her a cup of tea.

'It'll have to be Friday,' Harry said. 'I'm supposed to be working all this week.'

Alison smiled at him, drinking her tea.

The heat was awful all week.

Harry's grandfather coughed and sweated in the small yard. When she wasn't at the laundry, his mother listened to the wireless with the sound turned right up and the windows wide open. On the sands, trippers waded into the sea, wallowing up to their necks to escape the brilliant sunshine. There were fights every night on the promenade, and when the pubs shut, gangs of drunks roamed the streets, singing and drinking out of bottles.

Harry didn't mind the heat.

He was thin and bony, and had his hair cut short so that when he sweated it wasn't unpleasant. He went for swims most afternoons, and washed himself down in the yard when the little black flies crawled into his ears and on his skin. He hardly ate, and at the fairground, lived on iced lemonade.

'You are lucky, Harry,' his mother said one night as she fanned herself with a magazine. 'You got your dad's build.'

His grandfather grunted miserably when she said that to

him. Sullen and bad tempered, he was so ill with coughing over his cigarettes he spent most of the week in bed.

It was on Wednesday morning that he happened to see Florence Eliot.

He had finished with the lines and was walking down to the promenade. Crowds were already queuing at the pier to get tickets for the next show. Harry went and looked at the display photographs. A notice at the pier entrance said that before the show began, Miss Eliot was giving five free tickets so that people could check that she continued playing between performances. The five tickets had to be won on a tombola run by two of the young men in red tuxedos, and taking a chance, Harry won the fourth ticket.

He was led through the ornate pier entrance with the other winners and out along the pier to the pavilion at the far end. At the doors, one of the young men opened a window, and they gathered round and peered into the immense ballroom. Chairs were arranged in rows ready for the next audience, and up on the stage, a woman sat at a white piano, playing a slow waltz and being given drinks by one of her companions. The young man in the tuxedo allowed them to watch for several minutes, and before they left, the woman turned and waved, keeping just one hand on the piano. They walked back down the pier, and the crowds at the gate cheered.

When he told Elaine, she said it sounded beautiful.

'Nobody could play all night,' he said. 'You'd get cramp. You'd die, without sleep.'

'You're just a misery,' Elaine laughed, and told him she had no time to argue.

After the film, he walked with Alison to Grant's chippy. She wanted to go to Ted & Blue's, but he insisted they go and see Mr Universe. In the cinema, he had refused to kiss her, pretending he wanted to watch the film. He had nearly fallen asleep, tired and bored by the story, indifferent to the loud music.

When they got to Grant's he bought chips and mushy peas

and scraps, telling Alison he couldn't afford fish. They sat at one of the formica-topped tables, and he chatted with the lads behind the counter. There was always part-time work to be had at Grant's, and he usually knew somebody there. You could sit at one of the greasy tables for as long as you liked and nobody ever thought of it as a café.

Alison ate her food silently. When Harry asked her if she wanted tea, she shook her head without speaking. He blushed, and got himself a drink. As he ate, he stared round the walls at the faded posters. They were all photographs of Derek Grant in his days of fame. He had won the local Mr Universe contest in 1937, and the posters showed a huge man rippling with muscles and body oil, scowling into the camera. After the war, some of the posters had been used for advertising and had 'Grant's Fisheries' and the address printed at the bottom. A few of them were still around town, yellowing and showing out-of-date prices.

Not that Derek needed to advertise. He was one of the best fish fryers for miles, and people queued up waiting for him to open.

'I eat 'em meself, so they 'as to be good,' he sometimes said, and he helped himself all night, sitting behind the counter on a small stool, watching his customers with his tiny, grey eyes.

He was enormous.

'Eighteen stone,' Harry's mother said with amazement, coming home one night with fish and chips. 'He must be eighteen stone. And he looks like a bloody woman.'

Motionless behind the counter, he sat and stuffed himself with his own food, the rolls of fat bursting his shirt buttons, his breasts like an old woman's wrinkled female dugs, his long hair matted with sweat and stale hair oil.

But you didn't laugh at Mr Universe, even when he tried to push his hand inside your trousers. He had a temper like hot fat. If he caught you laughing, he might break your neck.

They finished their food and walked back down the promenade.

The illuminations were still on, and the coloured lights reflected in the dark water, flickering up and down as the tide lapped against the seawall. On the pier, people were dancing to Florence Eliot's music, and the big wheel spun and glittered against the sky, turning slowly above the noisy fairgrounds.

He wondered what Elaine was doing.

In one of the shelters, they sat down, and Alison took a small mirror from her handbag, straightening her neat fringe and frowning into the glass. Harry slumped against the wall, waiting for her to finish. When she turned to kiss him, he held her roughly in his arms, unfastening her blouse and trying to push his hand under the silk material of her brassiere. Unhappily, she let him touch her, hardly moving as he stroked her breasts. From the pier, they could hear the piano, and the sound of the audience applauding.

'I'm tired,' she said when Harry sat back and moved his arm.

'Yes.'

'Don't be angry.'

'I'm not.'

Together, they sat and listened to the music.

'She can't play,' Harry said. 'Anybody knows that.'

Alison glanced at him in surprise.

'She's a big star,' she said, trying to stroke his hand.

He laughed, pursing his lips in contempt.

'What's she doing in this dump then?'

'Harry!'

'Well, you think it's a dump, don't you? You can't wait to get away.'

'Don't say that.'

'You can't.'

She said nothing, staring at the ground.

Harry glared at her in sullen anger. He felt hot and miserable. He wanted to get up and walk out of the shelter.

'You believe she plays all night, don't you?' he sneered, nodding towards the pier.

'I don't know, Harry.'

'You believe it.'

'I haven't seen her,' Alison said very quietly.

'They use records,' Harry said with a sneer, staring defiantly out towards the estuary. 'They just use records, in case anybody listens overnight.'

Alison looked up at him and smiled.

'How do you know?' she said.

'Obvious.'

'But how do you know?'

'We can easily bloody check,' he shouted, turning on Alison with a sudden fury. 'Easiest thing in the world.'

She stared at him in surprise. Her face was flushed with pain.

She waited for him to go on, watching him with a careful smile, and when he grinned suddenly, they both started laughing, feeling ridiculous, sitting in the shelter, looking at each other for a long time, not knowing what to say.

But he had said it was easy to check, and Alison wasn't happy until he told her how. They fetched a strawberry whip from a small café, and then went back to the shelter and sat hand in hand, kissing in the darkness as Harry explained about the pier, Alison eager and excited, letting him unfasten her blouse and kiss her pink nipples through the brassiere.

'It'll be safe?' she whispered when he told her they might have to climb over the gates to get on the pier, and he laughed quietly, kissing the strawberry whip from her mouth, pushing her back against the hard wood of the seat.

'We'll not be long,' he said. 'Not if she's playing records.'

Alison kicked him, very hard, on the shins, and her giggles echoed in the shelter.

'And if she isn't?'

Harry glanced at his watch and groaned as she started to unfasten his trousers.

'Well, you'll want to stop and listen then,' he laughed. 'Won't you?'

*

The gates weren't locked. They stayed on the promenade until gone midnight and then walked up to the pier and stood by the ticket office in the main entrance. One push, and the gates swung slowly open.

'Must have forgot,' Harry whispered, holding Alison's hand and leading her out beneath the rows of illuminations.

Coloured lights were strung on either side of the pier. Over the entrance, an electric sign hummed with hundreds of bulbs, FLORENCE ELIOT shimmering in letters a foot high. In the pier pavilion, lights flickered through the tall windows.

'It's not a record,' Alison giggled when Harry stopped and told her to listen to the music. 'You can tell she's playing.'

'You'll see.'

They walked nervously along the side of the pavilion, and round to the back of the pier.

It was through a window to the rear of the building that they saw the piano player.

She was sitting at her piano, facing the windows to the left of the stage. In a silver candelabra, six candles burned on the piano. The main lights of the pavilion were out, and in the darkness, the candle flames flickered, tiny in the vast emptiness of the ballroom. Beside the piano, one of the young men slept in a canvas chair, his mouth wide open.

Florence Eliot was playing the piano.

A slow waltz, melancholy in the night silence, drifted out above the warm sea.

As she played, she rocked steadily backwards and forwards. Her back was held rigid. Her hands touched the keys and she winced with each note. Her mouth hung open, and she moaned through clenched teeth as she played.

Harry watched for only a few seconds longer.

Alison was crying, clinging to his arm. He saw the young man go over to the piano and pour two drinks from a large flask. He watched him give the pills to the woman, and then sit with her on the narrow piano stool, gently massaging her back. He watched the woman's face, white as the wax candles, her eyes bruised and exhausted, her smile like a clown's, made up for a carnival.

Harry called to see Alison the following week, and Dr Milburn came to the door. He invited Harry into the study and told him Alison was on holiday, staying with family in Yorkshire. She had been working hard for her exams, and deserved a rest before university. He laughed jovially when Harry asked if she was still upset about the piano player, and said he was sure she would be all right. 'She'll be in touch when she gets back from holiday,' he said, seeing Harry to the gate. 'I'm sure she'll send you a postcard.'

Nineteen

'We'll have a day off,' Elaine said one night when she was feeling fed up. 'You can show me round the fish docks.'

'What for?' Harry said, surprised.

'I can't work here for ever. Mildred shuts down in October.'

Harry hadn't been near the fish pontoons for months. He occasionally met Arthur after work, or went drinking in one of the fishermen's clubs. Mostly, he kept well away.

'You must be soft,' he said caustically. 'You'll never stand the fish docks.'

'The filleting sheds then. There's allus work there.'

'I'll take you to see Arthur.'

'I've seen Arthur.'

'All right, but you'll not like it. We'll go and see Frank Rudd. He'll maybe get you a job.'

'Who's he?'

'He works for one of the trawler companies.'

'A fisherman!'

'He used to be a skipper. He's retired now. He's a ship's husband.'

'You what?'

'A ship's husband.'

'What's that?'

'Hang about and I'll show you.'

They went down to the docks about a week later.

Harry told Mac he wouldn't be in for the day, and cycled up to Mildred's early the following morning. At five o'clock, Elaine came out of the back door, pushing Margaret's bicycle. She yawned, rubbing the sleep out of her eyes.

'You'll love working on the docks,' Harry laughed, teasing her.

'How do you mean?'

'Starting at five-thirty.'

'Not everybody.'

'Them that keeps their jobs.'

As they cycled through the empty streets, he told Elaine about Frank's job.

'A ship's husband looks after the ships when they're in port,' he explained. 'He sees they're all right for provisions and gear. Frank signs the crews on as well, but that's usually done by a ship's runner.'

'Why does he do it then?'

'Because he's so efficient.'

'Clever sod.'

'It's right. Herbert says he's the best ship's husband the port's ever known.'

'Don't you like him?'

'I like his grammar,' Harry grinned. '"Fuckin' blind man could be a ship's husband," Frank says. "These modern fuckin' diesels, they're so fuckin' mechanised, you order everything by fuckin' numbers."'

'Harry!'

'S'fuckin' true,' Harry laughed, swerving into the gutter as Elaine pushed him.

'You'll get us arrested.'

'You know what he told me once?'

'No.'

'He said he knew the fishing grounds better than his own street. Better than his own garden, his missus used to reckon.'

'Why?' Elaine asked.

'Because he was away so much.'

'They all say that.'

'It's true.'

They reached the dock gates and got off their bikes, wheeling them over the bridge that led down to the main quays. In the docks, they could see the masts of dozens of trawlers, moored alongside the market waiting to be unloaded, and up on the market roof hundreds of seagulls, warming themselves in the early sun.

'Why do you like him?' Elaine asked.

'He's a good bloke.'

'But why?'

'He was the one who came and told us when my dad drowned.'

They walked on across the bridge, the chains on their bicycles whirring in the dawn quiet.

'He used to be on the coal-burners,' Harry said, leading the way down a side-road to the quays. 'He always liked coal-burners. They had steam, you see. It was a bit rough on the trimmers and engineers, heaving all that coal around, but if the ship started icing up they could turn the hoses on and clear the worst off the decks that way. On the diesels, the deckhands have to get out on the whaleback and hack at the ice with axes. That's how Jack lost his hand.'

Elaine pulled a face.

'That's horrible.'

'Least he's alive.'

On the main quay, they dumped their bikes in the entrance of the building where Frank worked, and walked up the wide stairs. Harry's boots clattered on the concrete steps. Elaine was wearing plimsolls, old slacks and a jumper. They were going to cycle out to her parents' house after the market so that she could get some fresh clothes.

'What do I call him?' Elaine whispered.

'Skipper.'

'Why?'

'Because he was one, you daft sod.'

At the end of a long corridor, they went into the small office Frank Rudd used and Harry pushed a swivel chair forward for Elaine. He got a hard chair from the corridor for himself, and sat and watched the old skipper, who was wheezing and bellowing down the radio handset to one of the trawlers out at sea.

'Two freshers this morning,' Frank was saying, lounging back in the fishing chair he'd brought with him from the bridge of his last ship, pulling at a cigarette that seemed to be falling apart. He waved cheerfully to Harry and half-bowed to Elaine, lifting himself awkwardly out of his chair.

'Bleedin' heat here's terrific,' he shouted down the line. 'Mebbe you should lay to, Len, keep the trip fresh? Over.'

In the small cluttered room, the answering voice echoed clearly, better than a telephone call across town.

'That what the gaffers want, Frank? Catch the Wednesday market, is that it? What time's high-water? Over.'

'Four-twenty-eight,' Frank answered without glancing at the tide charts on the wall by his desk. 'I'll check with the boss and tell you this afternoon.'

'They spend half their lives at sea talking on the radio,' Harry whispered to Elaine while they listened. 'Makes 'em feel in touch.'

'What's he on about now?' Elaine whispered back.

'The catch. Most of these ships use ice to keep the catch fresh. That means they have problems in the summer. The fishing's easiest then, but the price never holds. If they come in during daylight heat and spend hours moored at the market the whole catch might end up condemned.'

'So they stay out at sea?'

'That's right.'

'But isn't it hot there too?'

'Course it is. But nobody knows how long they've been out there, do they?'

'That it then, Len?' the skipper was saying now into the handset. 'Will confirm this afternoon if yer to lay to, and we'll see the gaffers about the doors. Over.'

The skipper out at sea repeated the message, and after a few savage exchanges about fishing quota figures, Frank signed off and replaced the handset.

'Well now, Harry,' he grinned, leaning across his desk and shaking Harry's hand vigorously. 'And how are you this morning?'

'Fine, Mr Rudd, thanks.'

'Who's this you've brought to cheer me up?'

Harry introduced Elaine and explained that she was looking for a job on the docks.

'You're not, lass?'

'Yes I am,' Elaine said, shaking Frank's nicotine-stained hand and keeping his level stare.

'You think you can stand the smell?'

'Can't be worse than where I work now.'

'And where's that, pet?'

'Mildred's, on the prom.'

'You'd better not let her hear you say that,' Frank beamed at her delightedly.

'No, I'd better not,' Elaine said, freeing her hand.

'Are you from round these parts, Elaine?'

'Yes,' she lied, and Harry shifted uneasily in his chair, seeing Frank register the difference in her accent.

'And I suppose you'd like to look round the market while you're here?' Frank grinned.

'That'd be lovely.'

'Right then, let's get down there. See what the buggers are up to. There's a trawler just unloading. The *Newcastle*. We'll go and have a look how they're getting on. Should just be in time for the market. All right?'

'Fine.'

Getting up from his desk, he moved quickly round the cluttered office and out into the long corridor that ran the length of the main building. The building was still empty, and as he walked down the corridor his heavy boots echoed in the dawn stillness. Along the walls of the corridor, in tall glass cases, stood models of every trawler that the company had ever owned, right back to the sailing smacks that used to fish the Dogger Banks in fleets in the 1880s. Frank passed the models without a glance, Harry and Elaine struggling to keep up behind him.

Out in the early-morning warmth, he led the way quickly along the cobbled road towards the huge fish market off number one fish dock. Despite his thickening paunch and the wheezing in his chest, he still moved with the energy and lightness of a man half his age.

'I'm sixty-seven,' he beamed at Elaine when she asked him how old he was.

'You're not.'

'I am, lass, and on this market every morning an hour before anybody else in the company. Isn't that a fact, Harry?'

'It is.'

'Why's that?' Elaine asked.

'Somebody's got to sort the buggers out. They'd rob each other blind if I wasn't here to stop 'em.'

'What was that about doors, Frank?' Harry asked, holding on firmly to Elaine's arm.

Frank groaned.

'*Gainsborough*'s for'ard door's been giving trouble for weeks. Len asked me to get a new set, but you know what the gaffers are like. Tight-fisted buggers. They won't spend a farthing they don't have to. I'm trying to find a good spare set.'

'What's doors?' Elaine asked, out of breath with trying to keep up.

'Don't you know, pet?' Frank grinned.

'No.'

'And you coming from round here! Otter boards, some folk call 'em. They keep the mouth of the trawl open. Can't fish without 'em. Despite what gaffers think.'

'Can't you just tell them?' Elaine said, sounding surprised.

'Tell them?'

'Tell them what to do.'

Frank roared with laughter and winked at Harry.

'I would,' Elaine said, glaring at them both.

'I bet you would, pet. Just like my missus.'

At the top end of the market, they started along the quay, the harbour water oily and deep to their right, several trawlers moored alongside, their mooring ropes knocking against the bulwarks. The *Newcastle* was at the far end of the market, still being unloaded.

'How's the catch?' Harry asked, holding on to Elaine's arm as she slipped on the greasy cobbles.

Frank shrugged.

'Should be all right. She came in on the three-forty tide. Trouble is, she spent several hours in coastal waters. Doesn't do the fish any good. And you know Ronnie Lewis. Kept complaining about duffs.'

'What's duffs?' Elaine asked.

'Marine growths,' Harry explained. 'Foul, putty-coloured things. They're big as footballs, some of them, and covered with sharp spikes. Tear the trawl to shreds.'

'And the catch,' Frank grunted.

Harry's father always said you could tell when you were picking up duffs because the gutters in the fish pounds kept sucking their fingers to remove the spikes. They were a fisherman's nightmare, dragged up by the ton in the wide mouth of the trawl, only to be thrown back by the gutters after damaging both the net and the catch.

'The trouble is,' Frank said, 'you don't get duffs where the *Newcastle*'s been fishing. They're something you usually pick up in the White Sea, and even then only on certain grounds.'

'Well, what's he say it for then?' Elaine said impatiently. 'It's stupid.'

'He was probably hinting at the quality of the catch,' Harry said, squeezing her arm. 'Making out the quality's not much good. Duffs.'

'And quality's the last thing I need to be worried about,' Frank said cheerfully. 'There's already a bit too much codling and saithe for the gaffers' liking, and if the merchants get to hear talk about quality, the price could drop through the bottom of the floor.'

'I still don't know what you're going on about,' Elaine said bad-temperedly.

'They always try and get away with a few boxes,' Frank explained. 'Make out the fish are off, then sell 'em to their friends afterwards. It's just a way of making a bit of extra money. Normally, we take no notice.'

'Oh.'

'But this sounds more serious. A bit more organised. And I'm fucked if I'm having that,' he said with a big grin at Elaine. 'I'm fucked if I am.'

'But what can you do about it?' Elaine asked him.

Frank laughed and gave her a broad wink.

'You just watch me, pet. You just watch me. They won't know what's hit 'em.'

Twenty

When they got to the *Newcastle* berth they stood on the quay and watched the lumpers working at the catch. 'Pneumonia jetty' local people called the quay, and at six o'clock on a January morning you knew why, with a cold wind slicing off the North Sea and the snow scurrying across the big open market. But this morning there was hardly a breath of air, and flecks of pale pink coloured the sky and reflected in the oily surface of the dock as the gulls up on the market roof wheeled and screamed their excitement, diving down at every glimpse of fish.

Ronnie Lewis was still on the *Newcastle* bridge, arguing with one of the deckhands, but the mate, Mick Glover, nodded and walked over.

'Fuckin' hot, Frank,' he cursed, wiping the sweat off his face with the back of a tattooed arm and grinning at Elaine. At twenty-three, his face was nearly as brown as Frank's, but without the hardened polish that made Harry's grandfather's face shine like gnarled mahogany. He had a slouching walk, and wore thick gold ear-rings like a lot of the younger fishermen.

'Showing the lass how we slave, are you?' he grinned.

'Shouldn't you be in the hold?' Frank snapped, letting his irritation show. 'The catch is the mate's responsibility, you know that. You can't trust these bastards,' he added, with a nod towards the lumpers.

'Right y'are, skipper,' Glover laughed with a nasty smirk, taking a packet of cigarettes from his trouser pocket and offering one to Frank. 'I slipped the foreman a few quid. Shouldn't be no bother. For what it's worth. Want a cigarette, darling?'

Elaine took two cigarettes from the packet.

'Thanks,' she said, handing one to Harry and waiting for him to light it.

Glover shrugged, ignoring Harry. With a grin, he lit Frank's cigarette for him, and then walked casually back towards the lumpers who were laughing and fooling round the conveyor-belt.

Frank sucked a mouthful of smoke deep into his throat and spat into the harbour.

'He's a vicious sod,' he said to Harry, 'but he knows about fishing.'

Ronnie Lewis was still busy on the bridge, and Frank watched the lumpers on the quay impatiently. Years ago, the fish had to be manhandled up from the hold and out on to the dockside, with the mate and a deckhand down below to make sure there was no fiddling. Now a mechanical conveyor-belt was lowered into the hold and the fish were carried up and on to the market on a continuous belt to the bench where the lumpers sorted them into size and species for boxing.

'Fuckin' woman's job,' Frank muttered under his breath, stubbing his half-finished cigarette out on the quay.

On the *Newcastle*, Ronnie Lewis seemed to have finished bollocking the deckhand, and as the man clambered off the ship and walked unsteadily along the quay towards the transport café at the top end of the market, Frank scowled and lit another cigarette.

'Drunk,' he said briefly, glancing after the swaying figure. 'You be all right while I go on board?'

'Fine,' Harry nodded.

'Can't we come?' Elaine asked. 'I've never been on a trawler.'

'More than my life's worth, pet,' Frank laughed. 'Women on trawlers. You stay and watch the unloading. I shan't be long.'

'That's daft.'

'Aye, but it's true.'

With a grin, Frank climbed down over the bulwarks by

the for'ard gallows, and met the skipper at the foot of the narrow bridge-steps. They could hear him cursing and saying something about Glover. On the quay, the lumpers yelled and whistled, laughing as one of the men ducked beneath a hail of melting ice. Glover joined in the laughter.

'I can't stand blokes like that,' Elaine said nastily. 'Wearing ear-rings.'

'He's all right,' Harry laughed.

'Yeah, if you're not looking.'

Harry shrugged and watched the unloading.

Down in the fish hold, men yelled obscenities at each other as great lumps of ice crashed over the conveyor-belt to the floor and shattered into melting fragments. In the dawn sunlight, huge two-stone cod slipped and wallowed up the machine belt, their gutted stomachs open to the morning air, their vacant eyes staring with a flat, lifeless reproach. Reaching out a hand to the conveyor-belt, Harry touched one of the passing cod, its mottled skin dark green and fresh as if straight from the bottom of the sea, its gaping stomach clean from the gutter's swift knife.

'It's Arthur,' Elaine suddenly said, clutching his arm and pointing across the market.

'What?'

'Over there.'

Harry turned, and Arthur was already walking towards them, leaving his barrow and fastening the white coat that all the merchants' men wore when they were working.

'What're you fuckers doing?' he grinned, punching Harry's arm and smiling at Elaine. 'You're not signing on, Elaine?'

'What?'

'Female deckhands!'

'They won't even let me go on board,' she laughed.

'Quite right too. All right, mate?'

'Just having a look round,' Harry said.

'I bet. Frank worried about this lot?'

'Yeah.'

'Too many saithe. And codling,' Arthur nodded solemnly.

136

'Cod looks all right,' Harry said, glancing across at one of the lumpers who was playing with a large cod, pretending to drop it into the filthy waters of the dock. The men seemed to sense him watching, and one of them joked crudely with Mick Glover as they got on with the sorting. He could see them talking about Elaine.

'Lot of pale, they reckon,' Arthur said. 'Got it mixed in though, I expect. Hoping nobody notices.'

When cod began to lose their dark green colour they were near to going off, and if that was spotted a whole catch could be condemned. On the freezer-trawlers, it wasn't a problem. On the freshers, it could turn a profitable trip into a disaster. You needed a mate who really knew what he was doing to avoid that. Get the pale fish mixed in cleverly with the good and keep the lumpers busy. Slip them a backhander to make sure the fish was properly displayed on the market.

'You going to have a cup of tea?' Arthur asked, looking at his watch. 'I've got time.'

'Better wait for Frank.'

'Please yourselves.'

'We might see you tonight.'

'You might.'

Arthur went off to collect his barrow, and they stood for some minutes, watching the lumpers sort the fish and pack them into boxes ready for the seven-thirty auction. As the last of the fish were unloaded, Frank climbed off the ship and came back along the quay towards them.

'What's going on?' Elaine whispered, pushing her arm through Harry's and leaning against his shoulder.

'They're trying to work a fiddle,' Harry said.

'I know that.'

'Just watch. See what Frank reckons.'

Glover grinned when Frank came up.

'All right then, skipper?' he said, his fair hair knotted in tight curls round his face, his eyes too close together and bruised with tiredness.

'They used to do this by hand,' Frank said absent-mindedly. 'Not like gutting in a force ten gale, is it?'

Glover laughed, nodding and scratching the back of his neck.

One of the lumpers came over from the gang by the conveyor-belt and nodded cheerfully to Frank.

'Mornin', skipper,' he grinned.

'Gang foreman,' Glover explained.

'Got some rough stuff here,' the man said, pointing over to the side of the quay. He took them across to the boxes and they stood looking down at the pale, swollen fish. 'Bit rought that, mate,' the man repeated, winking at Glover.

It was an old trick, to put a few roughs on top of a good box and claim they wanted condemning. The fish underneath would be perfect, prime cod, probably the best of the catch.

Over by the conveyor-belt, Harry could see another twenty or thirty boxes lined up.

'Looks rough all right,' Glover agreed. 'You going to say anything?'

The lumper grinned and shook his head doubtfully.

Suddenly, Frank seemed to lose his temper.

'You're not buying that, are you?' he snarled at Glover.

The two men looked at him, Glover's smile fading and the lumper watching them both impassively.

'You're not falling for that trick, are you?' Frank went on, giving the first of the boxes a sharp kick.

'He says anything, we could lose the whole trip,' Glover said, keeping his voice quiet.

Frank laughed.

'I thought you gave him his backhander. There's good fish underneath that rubbish,' he said, pointing at the boxes. 'Fuckin' best of the trip, I shouldn't wonder.'

'Keep it quiet, Frank,' Glover said with a laugh, glancing across at the other lumpers.

But Frank ignored him and faced up to the lumper, giving the box another savage kick that moved it slightly towards the edge of the dock.

'You want me to get rid of them for yer?' he snarled viciously, clenching his fists and looking the man straight in the face. 'You want me to kick it in the fuckin' dock for yer, bein' as it's such rubbish? Or mebbe I should just take a look underneath.'

The lumper glanced at Glover, his eyes almost expression-less, the corners of his mouth twitching in a nervous grin.

'Stay out of it, Frank,' Glover hissed. 'You'll ruin the whole fuckin' deal, you soft bastard.'

Over by the conveyor-belt, other men in the gang were watching, and Ronnie Lewis was making his way from the deck of the *Newcastle*, puffing cheerfully at his pipe but moving quickly.

'Will you pack it in?' Glover went on nastily, gripping Frank's arm and twisting at it viciously. 'Go and warm your fuckin' armchair, for Christ's sake.'

But Frank was laughing in his face.

'All right?' he said to the lumper, and the man nodded unhappily.

'Right.'

Before Lewis could reach them, Frank turned and walked away from the quay.

They made their way to the top of the market.

There, a second gang of lumpers were setting out the catch ready for the auction. Haddock and saithe and some mixed were in the first boxes, then codling, flatties and cod, all graded and weighed from the smallest up to the immense specimens that took the best price in every auction. By seven o'clock, the catch stretched the length of the market, and as the market clock chimed the hour dozens of white-coated merchants milled around the slippery floor, climbing up on to the stacks of fish boxes to check the quality and make notes of the fish they wanted to buy.

'You still after a job then, pet?' Frank said as they reached the top of the market.

'Yes, I am.'

'Not put off by all this fiddling?'

'No,' Elaine grinned.

'I'll put the word out then. You'd best be on the processing. Ross, Eskimo Foods. If there's anything going, I'll get a message to Harry.'

'Thanks.'

He shook Elaine's hand, then laughed, saying 'What the hell,' and kissing her firmly on the cheek.

'You watch this one though,' he said with a nod towards Harry. 'He's a smart bugger.'

'I will,' Elaine smiled.

They watched Frank go off to talk to one of the merchants, and stood together underneath the market clock to wait for the auction. At seven-thirty, the auction bell would ring and the salesmen from each catching company would arrive, swarming across the huge market, shouting loudly to the merchants, bustling to get the sale finished so that the barrow boys could load the fish on to hand-barrows and get it across to the sheds for the filleters.

'I didn't understand,' Elaine said. 'About the fish. Not really.'

'Oldest trick on the docks,' Harry grinned.

'I could see that.'

'Every trip loses a few boxes.'

'But there were dozens.'

'Exactly,' Harry agreed.

'And the skipper seemed to know.'

'He probably organised it. Dropped a few hints to get Frank worried. Take a cut when the stuff's sold.'

Elaine sighed, helping herself to one of Harry's cigarettes and staring round the huge market.

'What I don't understand,' she said, 'is why he didn't just sack them.'

Harry laughed, squeezing her hand and wrapping his arm round her shoulders.

'Because he doesn't want to lose a good skipper,' he said. 'Or mate. They both know what they're doing. And if you sacked everybody on the fiddle in this place there'd be nobody left. Making a fuss was just Frank's way of giving them a warning. They won't try it again.'

With a loud clang, the auction bell began to ring, and everybody moved towards the centre of the market.

'We'll watch this, then have a cup of tea,' Harry grinned, excited by all the noise and bustle.

'All right.'

'Then you take me home and feed me,' he said solemnly, kissing her on the side of the face.

'Oh yes?'

'Well, unless you can think of summat else we can do.'

Twenty-one

A white mist hung over the hills. In the distance, a tractor gargled through the heat, rinsing the air with its noise. Pheasants coughed and racketed above the fields.

'You are lucky,' Harry shouted as they cycled along the narrow lanes.

'What?'

'Living out here.'

'In a field?'

'You know what I mean.'

'You haven't seen the house yet.'

The farming was mostly stock, sheep and some cattle. The chalk hills made growing crops difficult. Through the haze, Harry could see sheep grazing, fields full of poppies and Queen Anne's lace. In the silence, the sound of their wheels hummed like bees.

They stopped at the village shop and bought chocolates for Elaine's mother.

'And how are you, Elaine?' the woman behind the counter smiled, pretending not to see Harry. 'We don't see much of you these days.'

'I'm fine thanks, Mrs Arden.'

'That's all right then.'

Outside the shop, there was a pond surrounded by chestnuts and weeping willows. Water-lilies clogged the banks, white in the brilliant sun.

'Mum'll be at the farm,' Elaine told him as they walked down a steep lane towards the houses. 'She works until four o'clock.'

Her father was spending the day at Lincoln market.

At the bottom of the lane, they stopped by a fence and watched a tractor swinging across a field. The narrow lane was enclosed by hawthorns and brambles. Red rosehips shone in the hedge. Far away, a cuckoo was calling, and cows mooed in the field, disturbed by the noisy tractor.

'That's it,' Elaine said, and pointed down the lane towards two houses, red-brick and with slate roofs.

'I don't know why you want to leave,' Harry said, looking up into the sun and closing his eyes. 'I wouldn't.'

She laughed shortly.

'You don't live here.'

When they got to the house, Elaine went upstairs to change and Harry wandered down the garden. The key had been underneath the doormat. He stood in the garden, and listened to the distant tractor, still bouncing over the rough ground. A cloud of dust trailed behind it. In a ramshackle shed, he found the toilet, and sat with the door open, feeling the air on his legs. The toilet stank. Flies crawled on the walls.

In the kitchen, Elaine was making some tea.

She was wearing her black skirt and a white blouse with the collar turned up. Her hair was much longer than when they'd met, still a mass of dark curls. She had her ear-rings on, gold against her tanned face, motionless as she watched the kettle. He stood behind her and kissed her neck, his hands on her full breasts. He tried to turn her and kiss the freckles on her nose, but she pushed him away, laughing about the kettle. When he sat down at the table, she poured the tea and got cups and saucers from a cupboard, ignoring his amused stare.

During the morning, they explored the lanes, crossing fields to get back to the village and having lunch in a tiny pub. Bread and cheese was all the pub could manage, and they sat outside, drinking lager and watching some children play by the pond, talking about the fish market on the docks.

Elaine insisted she wanted a job on the processing.

'You can work overtime,' she explained about the fish-finger factories. 'It's up to you how much money you earn.'

Harry laughed and told her she didn't know what she was talking about, she'd never been inside.

'Eight hours, and you've had enough,' he said.

His mother hadn't stuck it for five minutes, and she was used to working on the fishing.

They had another drink, and then strolled round the village.

In the Norman church, they stood in the aisles and looked up at the tall windows. Coloured glass made patterns on the stone floor. The wooden collecting bowl looked like an eye, hand-carved from blackened oak. At the font, Elaine splashed him with the freezing water, and ran out of the church screaming when he tried to get hold of her. In the churchyard, she hid among the immense yew trees, jumping with fright when he managed to get round behind her and slip his hand over her mouth.

They got back to the house by early afternoon.

The kitchen smelt of lavender and fresh bread.

In the hot silence, they stood by the table and kissed, and then Harry led her upstairs, asking her which bedroom was hers. It was a small room at the back of the house, overlooking the garden and fields. He opened the window and she lay down. As he unfastened her blouse, she kept her eyes open, watching him. When he kissed her nipples, she massaged the back of his neck, and smiled vaguely when he looked up at her.

'Is something wrong?' he whispered, stroking her flat stomach, the soft hair behind her ears.

'Do you mind?'

'No, course not.'

'It's my time,' she said, blushing.

'I don't mind.'

She leaned forward, and kissed him on the mouth. Her eyes were still open.

'I can pull you off,' she said, breathing close to his face.

'No.'

'Let me?'

'No.'

Clumsily, he pushed her back on to the bed, and lay down beside her.

'There's nothing wrong,' he said, listening to the birds in the lane, the cuckoo still calling across the fields.

On the wallpaper, he counted dozens of roses.

Each time he blinked, he lost his place.

On the pillow, Elaine slept quietly, her hair falling across her cheeks, her freckles golden in the sunlight from the bedroom window.

Tired out, he went to sleep.

They cycled back that afternoon.

From the edge of the chalk hills, they could see the dock tower. Behind the tower, sunlight glinted on water. A haze of smoke rose from the curing houses and factories.

'I'm glad we were alone,' Harry said, when Elaine said she was sorry he hadn't met her mother.

On the final hill, they freewheeled all the way to the bottom, the afternoon air warm on their faces, Harry balancing easily with his arms held out like wings.

'I'm flying,' he yelled as Elaine floated behind him.

Miles away, at the estuary, he could see a trawler steaming over Binks Sands.

With a yell of delight, he took the handlebars and pedalled on the flat, looking over his shoulder to make sure Elaine was still with him.

Twenty-two

Throughout August, the heat was awful.

A heat mist lay on the river for days. Foghorns seemed to be going day and night. Curlews called sadly along the morning shores.

Because of the sultry weather, the crowds poured into the fairgrounds, looking for relief.

Ugly fights broke out for no reason. Machines were broken into. The glass front on the laughing policeman was smashed open one night and the ragged uniformed figure kicked along the promenade by a gang of youths on a day trip from Sheffield. When Norman and several of the men chased after them there was a fight in the middle of the road, women screaming and frightened, police sirens wailing down the promenade through the crowds.

Norman ended up with a broken arm.

Late one night, as Harry was collecting the takings from the fruit machines, he saw a girl shouting at a tall, overweight man. She was screaming abuse. A group of lads stood with her. When the man started to shout back, she went for him, her nails clawing at his face. Harry locked the fruit machine he was emptying and made for the office to put the cash in the safe. By the time he got back out, the man was being held by two of the girl's friends while she clawed at his face and a youth with greasy sideburns kicked at him savagely from behind, aiming at the kidneys.

Before Norman or Les could do anything, they were dragging the struggling figure out of the fairground and across the promenade. He was still fighting when Harry saw them thump him over the railings and jump down to the sands after him, the girl leaning on the railings yelling and jeering, spitting nastily as they knocked him about.

When the police arrived, the inspector asked to see Mac and told him he'd better get things sorted.

'I'm not having this every night,' he warned.

'What do you expect me to do about it,' Mac shouted angrily.

'Just sort it out, Mac.'

'You sort it out.'

The noise of the fairground hummed in Harry's head even when he was asleep. He dreamed of being carried round by the waltzer, crowds of youths clinging to the backs of the bucket chairs, girls shrieking and laughing as the chairs swivelled and lurched to the booming music. The music thumped and throbbed from the waltzer and rocket rides all day, drowning the steady beat of rock 'n' roll in the juke box room. When Harry woke up in the morning, his mouth was dry and stale and his head ached. He sat with his mother and drank endless cups of tea, listening to Jack coughing in his bedroom. With the kitchen door open, he gulped in long breaths of hot air, his feet aching from the hours on concrete floors, his mind bruised with trying to keep awake and concentrate.

Towards the end of the month, Mac told him to take a day off.

'You can't manage,' Harry protested.

'We'll manage.'

Norman punched him lightly on the arm.

'You need a rest,' he said gruffly, 'not like us old men.' His face was sweating with tiredness, his shirt collar filthy. Harry wondered why he never bought a new shirt. He was wearing his thick cavalry-twill trousers and the belt round his waist had three new holes in it. 'Take young Elaine for a day out,' Norman grinned.

Mildred said she would be glad to be shot of her.

'Mooning about,' she snapped irritably. 'Make sure she comes back in a better mood.'

They walked along the promenade and out to the coast road. The heat shimmered above the sea. Gulls wheeled and floated along the shores, screaming angrily, searching for food. In the fields, cattle grazed or simply stood and stared into the heat, surrounded by long grass and clover.

'Clive's moving on soon,' Elaine said.

'That'll please Mac.'

'He thinks the police have spotted him.'

Harry said nothing. The police probably couldn't care less. They had enough to do at the height of the season without bothering about national service dodgers.

'He says he might go up the coast.'

'Across the river?'

'He's been all over, you know.'

'Yes.'

'I've been nowhere,' Elaine grumbled.

They walked on in silence. When they reached the huge lock at the end of the coast road, they sat down on the low concrete wall and Elaine opened the sandwiches. She had made sandwiches at Mildred's, and a flask of iced lemonade. The water in the lock splashed and echoed as she prepared the food. The concrete was cool from the water. Looking down, Harry couldn't see the water, it was so dark. The lock opened out into a wide canal that was supposed to take any flood water and prevent flooding. Between the low banks, the canal cut straight through the flat countryside, shining like glass towards the low hills in the distance.

'Are you going to move on, Harry?' Elaine asked, offering him a sandwich.

'What?'

'When the papers come?'

'They haven't written yet.'

'They will, won't they?'

'I suppose.'

'What'll you do?'

'I don't know.'

'Ask Clive.'

'Yes.'

'He knows all the tricks.'

Harry shrugged.

He didn't want to think about it.

Catterick seemed a long way away.

'I'm not a magician,' he smiled, helping himself to another sandwich.

'I think you are,' she grinned.

'Something'll turn up. There's jobs on the docks.'

'They can trace you then.'

'Not if you haven't got a national insurance number.'

'Who said that?'

'Clive,' he grinned.

They walked back in the late afternoon and had tea at the Winter Gardens. Elaine kept staring at the waitresses and giggling at their black dresses and white aprons.

'I'd like to look like that,' she said.

'No you wouldn't.'

'She's ever so smart.'

As they ate their tea, Harry saw Alison go past, cycling with one of her friends.

She didn't see him, and Elaine was too busy eating to notice.

A few days later, Clive said he might be moving.

Mac was livid.

'I told you the whole season,' he said angrily.

'I don't reckon on getting caught, Mac.'

'What are we supposed to do?'

Harry asked him why he needed to move.

'You feel like moving on.'

'Nobody knows you down here.'

'You never know.'

'Don't be stupid. You think the police care?'

'Can't be sure,' Clive said.

Harry gave up.

'Please yourself.'

'You just get restless,' Clive said. 'Need to keep moving.'

Harry watched him working at the housey-housey. He

chatted with all the women, smiling and charming them, cracking jokes into the microphone. As the women shrieked with laughter, he smiled, but his eyes were blank. He enjoyed their laughter, worked to make them enjoy themselves, then stared out of the fairground, not hearing the questions they shouted at him.

'You going to go on the dodge?' Arthur said derisively one night, sitting on the waltzer steps and drinking a bottle of light-ale.

'I don't know.'

'Not worth it, I reckon.'

'He gets around.'

'To see what?'

'Better than Catterick.'

Arthur shook his head.

'Well, I reckon it's fucking miserable,' he said.

They sat without speaking.

Harry felt as though he hadn't slept for months. When he could get to sleep, Jack woke him with his racking cough, stumbling downstairs in the middle of the night to get himself a cold drink. He spent more and more time in bed, propped against the pillows. His face had gone thin this summer, a sickly colour beneath the dark tan. He always seemed to be out of breath.

'How's the old feller?' Mildred asked him one morning when he was sitting in the café, staring out of the window.

'He's all right, Mildred.'

'I remember him when he first left the ships,' she said, standing by Harry's table with her hands on her hips.

'Oh yes?'

'He was drinking for days.'

'Yes.'

'Getting into fights.'

'I know all that, Mildred.'

'They miss it, you know, even if they hate it at the time.'

Harry finished his tea and got up. He was irritated by her

kindness. Jack just kept him awake. He walked out of the café, his eyes black with exhaustion.

On the juke box, somebody was playing 'Blue Suede Shoes'. Mac was checking the money in his office. Harry and Arthur stood at the front of the fairground, watching the lights bobbing at the estuary, the monotonous blink of the lighthouse. A soft breeze cooled the night air, and the mist had lifted. It was gone midnight.

Arthur was the first to see them, cycling along the promenade.

Alison was in front, her arms held straight out for balance. Her friend followed closely behind, wobbling in erratic circles. As they rode, they were both singing. 'Only You', in high-pitched, hysterical voices.

They rode past Happiland, ignoring Harry and Arthur.

At the top end of the promenade, they turned in front of Wonderland and began to ride round in a tightening circle, their voices carrying along the empty front, Alison's white dress shining in the clear moonlight. They carried on singing. As they rode, their voices seemed to lift in the darkness, high and clear in the warm silence.

When Mac came out of his office, he stood with his hands on his waist, staring at the two girls.

He put the lights out, and they were still there, the lamps on their bicycles two dots going round outside Wonderland.

Twenty-three

A crowd of them were sitting on the steps of the waltzer and leaning against the fruit machines, exhausted by the dry heat.

'I've known a hundred and ten in Madras,' Norman bragged. 'And that was in the shade.'

'Leave off, Norman,' Les groaned.

'We used to play football.'

Norman emptied his bottle of brown-ale and opened another with his teeth. His arm was still in a sling, the filthy pot covered with loving messages and obscene drawings.

'In Bangalore, you can see the Hindus walking on red-hot coals,' Norman said vaguely, staring down at his hands. 'During the festivals, people light candles, stick them on the walls round the grounds. I've seen men weep for rain.'

'Like Mac,' Les grunted, and they all laughed.

When the weather was fine, nobody came into the fairgrounds.

'I need rain,' Mac shouted one night, frantically losing his temper.

Locking the last of the change kiosks, Clive came and slumped down beside Harry. His hair had grown long by now, and he had it tied back in a short pigtail. Under the lights of the waltzer, his hair looked blond.

'He still here?' Norman ridiculed.

'Mac can't do without me,' Clive smiled.

'Still running,' Norman announced, ignoring him.

He lifted his bottle and drained it at one swallow, beer running down his chin and neck.

'I can't stand cowards,' he said, glaring short-sightedly round the fairground.

'He can do what he likes for me,' Les yawned, and struggling to stand up, strolled off towards Mac's office.

Sheila, one of the prostitutes who worked their end of the promenade, came in and sat down beside Norman.

'Christ, this heat,' she said, fanning herself with her hand.

'Ent you doing the clubs?' Norman asked her aggressively.

'When I'm ready.'

'Supposed to be your job.'

'Give us a rest, Norman.'

'Supposed . . .'

'Fuck off, will you?' she yawned.

'I could go and stop with my sister,' Clive told Harry. 'She wouldn't mind.'

'Where's she live?'

'Sheffield.'

'I thought you were from down south?'

'My parents got divorced. I grew up with Carol. She's a nurse.'

Harry watched Norman glaring bitterly at the prostitute.

He seemed to have been on edge ever since his arm got broken. Upset about something and spending most of his time emptying bottles of beer. His clothes had begun to smell, and his eyes were rheumy, swollen. Harry wondered if he had ever been married. In all the years he had been working on the fairground, Harry had never seen him go with a woman. He just did his work, glad to be there, and went back to his digs.

Elaine came in at gone midnight.

A taxi drove up and she got out, shouting goodnight and slamming the door.

Her heels clicked as she walked between the machines towards them.

She went straight up to Norman and took the bottle out of his hand, draining it thirstily, lifting her head right back. When she was finished, she took a deep breath and wiped her mouth with the back of her hand.

'You thieving bitch,' Norman glared, staring at her but not attempting to get up.

Elaine sat down on the waltzer next to Clive and started

telling a joke. She told the filthiest jokes Harry had ever heard, usually to do with farm animals.

Norman listened with a scowl on his face, his eyes glazed, his hand shaking as he opened a new bottle. When Elaine offered to show them what the kids on the farm used to do to dogs, he flew into a rage, telling her she needed a good belt. He seemed genuinely upset.

Elaine stuck her tongue out at him, and made a point of offering Sheila a cigarette, lighting it for her with a gold cigarette-lighter Harry had never seen.

Stumbling against the fruit machines, Norman stood up and steadied himself, clutching his bottle of beer.

'They should fetch the police to you,' he said angrily, leaning towards her and squinting as if he couldn't see. 'Mac should telephone the police.'

'You telephone,' Elaine laughed.

Harry wanted to get up and walk away.

He sat and stared miserably at the floor, listening to Norman's heavy breathing, Sheila's rasping laughter.

'You tell the old sod, darling,' Sheila croaked, coughing on her cigarette. 'You tell him.'

Norman staggered off towards the back of the fairground.

For some minutes, they all sat in silence, listening to his clumsy footsteps, the crash of the door as he went into Mac's office. When he'd gone, Elaine stood up and held her hand out to Clive. She was sweating. Harry looked up and he could see the sweat on her top lip, her eyes shining unnaturally. He could smell the brandy. She held Clive's hand and they walked to the rear of the fairground and got into one of the cars on the ghost train. Harry was left sitting with Sheila. She finished her cigarette.

'That's it then,' she sighed, grunting and getting to her feet. 'Round the fucking clubs.'

'See you, Sheila.'

'You don't want a bit of company, darling?'

'No, thanks.'

He glanced away, thinking about Elaine, watching the lights out at the estuary.

'I got a son your age,' Sheila sighed. 'He don't speak to me either.'

'I'm sorry.'

'That's all right, pet. You take no notice. She your girl?'

'What?'

'Showing off,' Sheila said, nodding towards the ghost train. 'No.'

'You take no notice. Not worth it, pet. No fucking different, one or another. 'Night.'

''Night.'

Arthur came over and sat down.

'Patrick's home,' he said. 'Been fishing off Greenland.'

'Easy weather.'

'He says they got becalmed,' Arthur said. 'Diesels went or summat. Just lay there, off Cape Desolation. Had to wait for an engineer.'

There was a shriek from inside the ghost train.

'They gone for a ride?' Arthur laughed, surprised.

Elaine cried again, and Arthur stood up.

'Leave it, Arthur,' Harry said. 'I'm going home anyway.'

Arthur watched him for a minute and then shrugged.

He turned and walked across to the ghost train. Harry stood up. He could hear Elaine giggling, and then there was silence. Arthur jumped up the wooden steps to the ghost train platform and went into the ticket office. Harry knew what he was going to do, but he couldn't move. He felt exhausted. Drained. He stood and waited.

When Arthur started the motors, the train lurched against its brakes and there was a quick shout from inside the tunnel.

The motors made a tremendous clanking noise in the empty fairground.

Over by the grand national race, Harry could see Mac and Norman rushing out of the office and starting towards the ghost train.

Mac was waving his arms.

Arthur did something with the controls inside the ticket office and jumped down off the platform, strolling back nonchalantly to stand beside Harry.

'Going home?' he asked.

'You can't leave them.'

Arthur laughed.

'Serve 'em right,' he said, taking Harry's arm.

'What the hell's going on, Arthur?' Mac shouted, rushing up and staring in panic towards the ghost train.

'Giving 'em a ride,' Arthur said.

Norman was stopped in his tracks, gasping for breath and struggling to tighten his trousers.

On the platform, the train rumbled to a halt. Elaine and Clive were sitting in the front car. Elaine was kneeling on the floor, trying to pull her clothes on. Clive had fallen back against his seat. When the train jerked to a halt, Elaine looked up and saw Harry. Her face was completely white.

She stared at him, struggling with her clothes.

'You bastard,' she shouted, fumbling with the belt on her skirt. 'Mean fucking bastard.'

Harry couldn't speak.

When she gave up trying to fasten the skirt, Clive made a move to help her and she pushed him away furiously. Tears were running down her cheeks, smearing her face with black mascara.

Turning away, Harry walked out of the fairground and went home.

Twenty-four

Harry was working in the juke box room.

The new Presley had been released at the end of August, and all day 'Hound Dog' and 'Don't Be Cruel' alternated on the juke box, a crowd dancing so close to the machine that nobody could select a different record. Fights and scuffles broke out as the narrow room got steadily hotter and the crowd more excited.

'It's driving me fucking mad,' Les complained, wanting Mac to call the police and turn them all out.

'Close your ears,' Mac snapped back, irritated by the music but not knowing what to do.

He told Harry to stay on the entrance, leaving him there most of the day.

'I trust you,' he grinned, patting Harry on the arm. 'Make sure there's no trouble.'

'How?'

'Use your charm.'

The music seemed to be hypnotising the crowd.

When 'Hound Dog' was on they danced in a frenzy, shouting and clapping their hands above their heads, chanting the words so that you could hardly hear the record. At the slurring, hot excitement of 'Don't Be Cruel', several girls sat in stunned silence, clutching photographs of the wild-looking American until 'Hound Dog' got them back on their feet. Some of the men were as bad as the girls, flushed and white-eyed with pleasure.

It was gone eleven when Ronald Timms and his friends came into Happiland.

'Only got another week, Harry,' Ronald said, slurring his words and wrapping his arm round Harry's shoulders. 'You going to let us in for free?'

'Course,' Harry grinned diplomatically, dropping the rope that was kept across the entrance.

'There's a good boy.'

The soldiers pushed their way into the darkened room.

'Thanks, mate,' one of them winked at Harry, grinding his knuckle into Harry's shoulder.

Harry watched them go inside and lifted the rope again.

'What's happening?' Mac asked him, coming out of his office.

'Nothing yet.'

'You go and get a break.'

'We'll be shut soon.'

'You've been at it all day. Go and have a drink.'

By the time Harry got back, the juke box room was nearly empty. Mac had turned the lights on, and the soldiers were standing round the juke box, stopping anybody using the machine. Ronald was slouching right in front of it, leaning back against the selector. Two of the soldiers were sitting down on the wooden benches, chatting with girls who hadn't left. The tall soldier with a weeping skin complaint was boasting about having the crabs, smirking at the young girls who were giggling at him in a corner.

'You know how they treat crabs, Harry?' Ronald shouted when Harry walked back into the room.

'No.'

'Doesn't know what they are, do you, mate?' one of the soldiers said, and they all laughed.

'Summat crawling up the sands,' the tall soldier sneered.

Harry sat down. He knew he couldn't walk out of the room now.

'Get 'em off wog women,' Ronald smiled unpleasantly. 'We all 'ad 'em.'

'Lovely women, wogs,' one of the soldiers sitting beside Harry giggled, his voice high-pitched and nasty.

'You know what they do?' Ronald said, staring coldly at Harry.

'Who?'

'Army doctors?'

Harry shook his head.

'They have this kind of needle. Got a blade at the end, sort of ridge. They stick it up your prick, give it a good turn, then open this ridge thing out. Scrape the crabs clean when they pull the needle out. Clean as a whistle. Ready for the next time.'

The soldiers seemed to find Ronald hilarious.

He beamed round at their laughter, thumping the tall lad on the back as he spluttered and coughed against the juke box. Pushing Ronald away, he spat on to the floor, and kicked the ground with the heel of his boot.

Clive walked in and stopped abruptly at the entrance.

He was holding the key for the juke box and two or three new records.

The soldiers watched him.

'I was going to do that,' Harry said quickly.

Clive stared at Ronald.

'That's all right, Harry,' Ronald said cheerfully. 'Going to change the records, are you, mate?'

'That's right.'

The soldier with the high-pitched voice giggled.

'Better do it then,' Ronald nodded. 'Can't stop a man working, can we, boys?'

Clive glanced at Harry.

His face was white.

He walked up to the machine and Ronald didn't move.

'Excuse me.'

'Oh, sorry, pal. In your way, am I?'

Ronald moved to one side and Harry saw the tall soldier with the scabbed face sidling along the wall towards the entrance.

Harry's legs were trembling.

Clive unlocked the front of the juke box and swung the door back. He knelt down and started to revolve the records so that he could remove the ones Mac wanted replacing.

'You had your papers yet, Harry?' Ronald suddenly asked, smiling at Harry.

'No, they haven't come.'

'Another couple of months?'

'Eighteen, are you?' the soldier sitting next to Harry asked.

'In December.'

'Come soon then,' the soldier nodded.

'Mine come a month early,' Ronald informed them, beaming happily.

At the juke box, Clive started putting the new records into the revolve.

'How about you, pal?' Ronald said.

Clive didn't look up.

'Not yet,' he said, struggling to fix one of the records.

'Not yet,' the tall soldier mocked, standing by the entrance.

'Get the records muddled sometimes,' Ronald nodded sympathetically.

'Yes.'

'You been home recent then?'

'How do you mean?'

'Not from round here, are you? Accent like that?'

Clive closed the door of the juke box and stood up. Harry could see his face in the light of the machine. He was sweating.

'Not from these parts?'

'No. My family . . .'

'Your what?'

'My sister lives in Sheffield.'

The tall soldier sniggered.

'He lives with his sister,' he told the others.

They all laughed, guffawing, watching Ronald.

Ronald stopped smiling.

'No fixed abode,' he said firmly, with a nod of his head. 'Definitely.'

Clive faced him, holding the old records in his right hand.

'Got a room behind the station,' he said. 'For the time being.'

Nobody spoke.

Harry felt the soldier to his left steadily moving closer towards him. He closed his eyes and clenched his fists, feeling his fingernails dig painfully into the palms of his hands.

'You finished, Clive?' Mac's voice suddenly came from the entrance.

Harry opened his eyes.

Mac was standing there, right next to the tall soldier. He beamed round the room cheerfully.

'All right, boys?'

'Fine, Mac,' Ronald grinned. 'Fine.'

'Lock up when you're finished, Clive,' Mac said and turned, smiling at Ronald.

They watched him go.

Clive and Ronald were still standing by the machine, facing each other.

Harry hardly saw Clive's hand move.

Suddenly the records were smashed against the top of the machine and Ronald was reeling back against the wall. The tall soldier leapt across the room and kicked Clive brutally in the kidneys, knocking him to the floor where he twisted quickly sideways out of the way and tried to scrabble to his feet before the second soldier could reach him. The soldier sitting next to Harry had lunged out before Harry saw what was happening, and as Harry hit the floor he felt his arm being jerked savagely behind his back and then his head slammed into the floor, the man sitting astride his shoulders and bashing his face into the rough concrete, taking the skin off his cheeks and jaw.

As Harry fought to break free, he saw Clive going backwards into the juke box and the glass front collapsing and splintering. Fragments of broken glass shot everywhere. Two of the soldiers had Clive by the arms, and as he writhed to get away, Ronald kicked him repeatedly between the legs, yelling and cursing as blood ran down Clive's face and he flailed to bend double away from the blows. The next minute, Norman was across the floor, smashing the pot on his broken arm into the back of Ronald's head. Ronald turned, and seemed to laugh. Harry saw the knife, flashing in the light of the juke box, and then Norman was on the floor and Clive was slumped against the wall, his hands clutching his stomach, blood seeping through his fingers.

With a final kick, the soldier on Harry's back leapt up and ran off after his mates.

By the time the police and ambulance arrived, Harry was unconscious.

Twenty-five

Harry's face stiffened as the wounds dried into scabs. The blood up his nose gradually cleared. He could hardly move his lips, grazed skinless by the pounding on the rough concrete. He couldn't eat or drink for two days, and lay in bed, listening to the wireless, his grandfather coughing in the room next door, his mother moving about downstairs. Out on the banks, September had brought the usual fogs, and the foghorns moaned all day on the river.

On the third day, his mother came into the room and said there was somebody to see him.

It was Elaine.

She sat down on the chair looking awkward and embarrassed.

'Are you going to have a cup of tea, love?' his mother asked, and Elaine smiled gratefully, nodding her head.

'Thanks very much, Mrs Kelam.'

'You'll have to drink it without Harry,' his mother said ruefully, and left them alone, chatting to Jack before going down to the kitchen to get the kettle on.

Elaine sat on the chair, looking down at her hands.

She looked as if she hadn't slept for days.

Her hair needed a wash, greasy and knotted with tight curls. Her fingernails were cracked and broken. When she saw him looking at her, she blushed and stared back defiantly, then suddenly looked away, not able to keep the sharp smile.

Harry leaned forward and touched her hand.

When she looked at him, he pointed to his lips and shook his head.

'You can't speak,' Elaine said, and bit her lips quickly, her eyes filling with tears as though she didn't want to listen to any more. She dried her eyes roughly and pushed her handkerchief back into her coat pocket.

'Norman's arm's broken in two places,' she said. 'They had to set it again. Take off the old plaster. They didn't think the drawings were very funny.'

After the fight, the police had arrived following an ambulance.

Timms and his friends had been picked up in one of the clubs down on the fish docks. They were blind drunk by then and put up no fight. According to Mac, Timms was going to be charged with assault.

Elaine sat quietly, fiddling with the sleeve of her coat. It was the same thin coat she'd been wearing at the beginning of the year when it was still winter.

She smiled at Harry but couldn't speak.

He noticed how thin her face was, the cheekbones jutting through the tanned skin. She wouldn't ever lose the tan, he thought, the masses of tiny freckles round her nose.

Clive was still in hospital.

'The knife went into his stomach,' Elaine said. 'Damaged the stomach lining. He was in intensive care at first. They reckon he'll be all right. They got his sister's address from his wallet. She came over, from Sheffield. She's staying in a guest house. I haven't seen him though,' Elaine said, shaking her head. 'I can't get in. They say I'm not family.'

She was crying again, sitting forward on the chair and sobbing without making a sound.

When Harry's mother came into the bedroom with the tea, she put the tray down on the floor and knelt beside the chair, holding Elaine in her arms and looking concerned at Harry.

'What is it, pet?' she kept on saying, but Elaine couldn't speak.

She just cried, as if she would never stop, rocking backwards and forwards in Harry's mother's arms.

Sitting up in the bed, Harry wet his lips and tried to speak, but the pain almost made him faint.

He sat and watched the two women.

Outside, in the street, a stray dog yapped frantically.

He was away from Happiland for a week, and then went back to work. He wanted to know what was happening. Elaine hadn't visited again, and when Mac called to see how he was, he was asleep.

'You should have woken me,' he told his mother, but she sat downstairs with Mac drinking tea and gossiping for hours, and wouldn't tell Harry what they'd talked about.

On the morning he went back, the fairground was almost deserted.

Norman was playing patience, sitting at the bagatelle tables. Les was doing his coupons, testing the draws out on a couple of the fairground workers. In his office, Mac sat smoking a cigar, staring unhappily at an open ledger.

'You want to come back?' he asked when Harry sat down.

Harry nodded.

It was still painful to speak, move his mouth. He hadn't eaten for a week, but was drinking weak soups and some medicine the doctor had prescribed.

'Sure?' Mac insisted.

'Course.'

Mac sighed.

'Most wouldn't,' he said sadly. 'Clear out, most lads. You're daft, Harry.'

'It wasn't much,' Harry said slowly.

'Tell that to Norman.'

Getting up from his desk, Mac filled the kettle at the sink and turned the gas on. He put out two cups. The smoke from the cigar filled the tiny room.

'What's happening to Clive?' Harry asked.

Mac shook his head.

'Mac?'

'He'll be in hospital a bit longer,' he said, not looking at Harry.

'And then?'

'Police want to see him.'

'He didn't do owt.'

'Not about that. They've charged your friends.'

'They're not my friends, Mac.'

'Grievous bodily harm.'

'And?'

'Trial will be this autumn.'

'What about Clive?'

'He'll be arrested.'

Harry stared at him in silence.

'Arrested for desertion,' Mac said abruptly.

He got up and walked to his office door then turned and came back. He sat down, crashing his chair against the wall. Trying to light his cigar, he burned his fingers on the match.

'Arrested?' Harry said.

'You heard.'

'But he could join up. Now, I mean. They've got him . . .'

'Not fit to serve,' Mac said, leaning back in his chair.

'What do you mean?'

'Even when he recovers, he'll not be fit to serve.'

'Then why . . . ?'

'For Christ's sake, Harry!'

'Why fucking arrest him?'

Mac got up and walked out of the room.

When Harry joined him, he was arguing with Norman about the cards.

'You're fucking cheating,' Mac shouted, his face bright red, banging the bagatelle table with his fist.

Norman stared at him in disbelief.

'So what?' he said.

'You can't cheat at patience.'

'Why the hell not?'

'What's the fucking point of playing. You just cheat yourself.'

'At least I win,' Norman shouted back, and flinging the cards down on the table, got up and stalked off to the other end of the fairground.

Behind the counter, Les hid the coupons and started rearranging the prizes.

Elaine wasn't at the café and Mildred didn't know where she was.

'Probably at the hospital,' she sniffed. 'Hoping to see the hero.'

Harry asked for a cup of tea and sat at one of the window tables.

The promenade was nearly deserted. Once the holidays were over, the fairgrounds were only busy at weekends. He drank his tea and watched a couple of bait diggers at the tideline.

It was early afternoon when Arthur turned up.

'You feeling better?' He grinned at Harry, sitting down and making a show of studying Harry's bruises.

'I'm fine.'

'You look horrible.'

'Thanks very much.'

'All them scabs.'

'Pity you weren't around.'

'Never get involved,' Arthur laughed. 'Tea please, Mildred. Where's the girls?'

'It's Margaret's day off,' Mildred said briefly.

'What about Elaine?'

Mildred sniffed again loudly and banged Arthur's cup down in front of him.

'Don't ask,' Arthur nodded. 'Right.'

'You're early,' Harry said as Arthur drank his tea.

'Not much in at the moment.'

Arthur looked awkward, avoiding Harry's eyes. He concentrated on drinking his tea and stared out of the window.

'Is that Herbert out there?' he asked casually.

'You can see it isn't.'

'Soon be back digging,' Arthur smiled. 'Season's nearly finished.'

There was a long silence.

167

Harry stared out of the window, and suddenly knew what Arthur was going to tell him.

'You've had your papers,' he said flatly, watching Arthur's face.

Arthur never moved.

'Arthur?'

With a shrug, Arthur looked down at the table.

'No,' he said.

Harry waited for him to go on.

'The fishing,' he said at last, and shook his head when he saw the expression on Arthur's face. 'You've signed up for the fishing.'

For a long time, neither of them spoke.

Mildred came across and filled their cups from the teapot.

Walking hurriedly, Norman came along the promenade, and disappeared into the pub next door to Mildred's.

'I can't face Catterick,' Arthur said at last. 'I just can't face it. I wouldn't survive.'

'Don't be stupid.'

'Blokes like Timms . . .'

'You'd survive longer than at sea.'

'So you're going to join up, are you?' Arthur said angrily.

'There's other things.'

'Like what?'

'You don't have to go on the trawlers.'

'And you don't have to go in the army,' Arthur said derisively. 'You want to wake up, Harry. We can't all be fucking magicians. And look what happened to him!'

They sat together for a long time in silence, then Harry got up and walked out of the café.

Later on, when he was working on the waltzer, his mother came down to the fairground, and told him Herbert Edlin had died.

Twenty-six

The morning of the funeral was bright and clear.

There were cars lining the street outside Herbert's house, and by the time they got to the cemetery, dozens more were following the procession. Along the funeral route through town, people stopped to pay their respects, old men taking off their caps, women admiring the flowers.

Harry and his mother went in George Bainbridge's car.

They had to help Harry's grandfather, he was so weak after the long summer.

'I'm all right,' he kept complaining, sitting uncomfortably in the back of the car. 'I can manage on my own.'

He could hardly walk.

At the grave, he stood and glared throughout the service, refusing to say the words.

When it was finished, he threw dried seaweed on to the coffin.

Back at the house, George offered to help him up to bed but he insisted on having a drink.

'Never seen a pal off yet without a drink,' he said aggressively. 'Not going to start now.'

Harry's mother went upstairs to get ready for work.

'She wouldn't have to if you got yourself a proper job,' Jack sneered at Harry.

George glanced at him nervously.

'Not now, Jack.'

'What?'

'Not now.'

'It's the truth, isn't it? Can't he stand telling the truth?'

'There's a proper time, Jack,' George muttered, handing him his glass.

Jack scowled into the brandy and swallowed it at one go. Harry refused the bottle.

'What's up? Aren't you going to drink to my friend?'

'He was my friend as well,' Harry said quietly.

'You shouldn't speak his name,' Jack sneered.

'You what?'

'You shouldn't speak his name.'

Finishing his own drink, George put his glass down and squeezed Harry's arm.

'I'd best be going.'

'All right.'

'I'll see you later in the week.'

At the table, Jack poured himself another glass.

'See you around, Jack.'

'You might.'

When the door closed, Harry took the bottle and put it back on the shelf by the range.

'What're you doing?' Jack scowled.

'You've had enough.'

'You say so?'

'That's right.'

Sitting down, Harry loosened his tie. He could hear his mother upstairs, closing her wardrobe door.

'You'll not make a fuss,' he said, glancing at his grandfather.

'You what?'

'You heard, Jack. She's upset enough as it is.'

'And I'm upsetting her?'

'You'll not, that's all.'

Jack grinned nastily.

'There's nowt wrong with your mother a good rest wouldn't cure. But she's not going to get that, is she?'

'You finished?'

'She's not going to get that, because you're too fucking idle to get yourself a proper job.'

'I've got a job,' Harry said angrily, whispering through his teeth.

'On a bloody fairground!'

'It pays good money.'

'Working on a fairground!'

'Piss off.'

'You idle sod. Layabout. If you had any guts you'd get on the fishing. That's where you earn money. On the fucking fishing. Not messing around with bleedin' tarts.'

'Shut up,' Harry yelled, banging the table and knocking Jack's drink out of his hand.

Delighted, his grandfather grinned at him.

'If you were a man,' he said, 'you'd do the same as your father. At least he didn't expect my daughter to keep him. But you're not fit to mention your dad's name.'

With a sharp cry, Harry smashed his grandfather's glass to the floor, and slammed out of the kitchen.

As he went down the yard, he could hear the old man laughing.

Up in her bedroom, his mother opened the bedroom window, and shouted after him down the street, calling his name as he turned the corner and ran across the waste land towards the railway embankment.

Twenty-seven

September was nearly over.

A few mornings after the funeral, Harry told Elaine that he was going out bait digging. He had a special order to get for George Bainbridge.

'I'll do you breakfast,' Elaine said. 'At the café.'

She was sleeping at the café now, in the back room where the previous owner had kept a small bed. Mildred had given up bothering.

At five o'clock, Harry met Arthur and they set out together across the sands.

It was Arthur's last day before sailing. His trawler was already berthed at the North Wall, and he would be signing on in the morning. They walked quickly over the ridged sands, their boots slapping in pools of water, Harry's bucket clanking against his leg.

'She'll not be there,' Arthur said when he told him about the breakfast.

'Doesn't matter.'

'You always go to Brown's.'

Ahead of them, the huge sky was cloudless and opal.

Swarms of seagulls squabbled above the tide, terns and curlews keerreeing along the tideline.

On Sanctuary Point, the coastguards would be changing shift, scanning the horizon with their binoculars, brewing fresh tea and checking the night's activity on the river. When you stood at the tideline, you could sometimes see the sun glinting off their powerful glasses.

They worked steadily for an hour and filled the bucket with good, fat worms.

'You know where to dig,' Arthur said, wiping the sweat off his forehead.

'Thank Herbert,' Harry said quietly.

'Herbert,' Arthur said solemnly, smiling up at the morning sky.

When they'd finished, Harry straightened his back and cleaned his shovel.

'Can you take 'em to George's for us?' he asked Arthur.

'If you want.'

'I'll go and see about breakfast.'

'I told you, she won't be there.'

'Still.'

They walked together back towards the promenade.

'I shan't come down tomorrow,' Harry said.

When a trawler sailed, friends and family usually went down to the docks, standing on the wooden pier beyond the lockpit to wave farewell. Crowds of children saw every ship off. Fishermen believed it was bad luck to go to sea with any silver, and they emptied their pockets to the children who swarmed around the quays.

'That's all right,' Arthur nodded.

'I've got another order,' Harry said.

Arthur punched him lightly on the arm.

'I said it's all right.'

Harry climbed the steps to the promenade alone, and found Elaine busy setting a table out in the middle of the road.

'We'll be able to see the tide,' she said when he laughed at her dragging chairs out of the café.

'We'll get run over.'

'Not this time of morning.'

He helped her lay the table with a red-and-white checked tablecloth and plates and cutlery from the café. Elaine warmed the plates over the grill and he got salt and tomato sauce from a cupboard behind the counter.

'Mildred's going to be furious,' he laughed as Elaine took sausages and heaps of bacon from the fridge. 'She'll murder us.'

'Stop fussing.'

Elaine finished the fry with some mushrooms she'd fetched from the market.

'I went down at five,' she chattered, serving the food on to plates. 'You get the best if you catch the first deliveries. Give us a hand with this.'

They had sausages and bacon and eggs, with fried potatoes and black pudding, and the mushrooms lightly grilled. The bread was still warm from the oven, and Harry guessed she'd stopped off at the bakery near the railway station. She must have been up before he went digging.

'Are you going to finish the season?' he asked as he cleaned his plate with a slice of bread and poured them both some more tea.

Elaine had heard about a job on the processing.

She shook her head, her mouth full of food.

'I don't know,' she said. 'See what happens.'

'There's plenty of jobs,' Harry told her. 'You'd have no trouble getting something.'

'I like it down here,' she smiled.

'So do I.'

The meal finished, they sat together and drank their tea.

The tide was far out, thundering in the distance. Clouds of birds wheeled over the sea. The September sunlight was pale and warm on their faces.

'I could live here for ever,' Elaine said with a big sigh.

Harry said nothing.

As the sun began to climb in the sky, he helped her get the table and chairs back into the café, and then they washed the things up together, happy in the empty café, the morning wireless droning on about what was happening in Aden.

'I've come to say goodbye,' Alison said.

She was wearing a green polo-neck jumper and pleated skirt. Her hair was pulled back behind her ears and she had small pearl ear-rings. She wheeled her bike into the yard and propped it against the kitchen wall.

Harry had seen her at the funeral, standing at the rear of the packed church.

'I was going to come and see you,' he said.

'I know.'

He felt uncomfortable, standing awkwardly at the kitchen table.

Alison smiled and sat down.

'You'll have been busy.'

'Yes,' he nodded.

'Aren't you going to sit down?'

'My mother's still at the laundry,' he said, and she laughed.

'Don't be silly, Harry.'

While she put the kettle on, he fetched more coal and heaped it on to the fire. The flames leapt at the back of the chimney and the range was warm.

He sat down, and Alison arranged the cups and teapot on the table.

'I'm going next week,' she told him. 'My father's taking me down.'

'You must be looking forward to it?'

'Yes, I am.'

He couldn't think of anything to ask.

It seemed a long way away.

'I've never been to London,' he said.

'You can get on a train.'

'Yes.'

'I'll meet you at King's Cross.'

His mother came home at four o'clock.

'I'm sorry about Mr Edlin,' Alison said.

'Yes. We saw you at the funeral. It was nice of you to go.'

The two women seemed easy together. Harry watched them, standing apart but friendly, familiar.

'Harry's embarrassed,' Alison smiled. 'He doesn't like goodbyes.'

'Well, it's not really goodbye, is it?' Harry's mother chattered. 'You'll be coming home, I'm sure.'

'Tell my father otherwise.'

They both laughed and Harry's mother hung her coat behind the stair door.

'You walk me up the road, Harry?'

He saw her up as far as the cinema, then said he had to go down to Happiland to see if Mac needed anything.

'I shall miss you,' Alison said.

They stood facing each other.

'I shall really miss you.'

There were tears in her eyes, but she couldn't help smiling.

She touched his hand lightly, and then kissed him on the cheek. He put his arms round her, but he felt cold, upset. She held him tight.

'I can't help being excited,' she whispered.

'I know.'

'Don't forget me.'

She cycled off, and he walked down the road to the promenade, his eyes blinded by tears. He couldn't see the sea.

Twenty-eight

At the end of September, Elaine came into the fairground one night and sat down on the steps of the waltzer.

It was a Saturday, the last busy weekend of the year.

She looked tired, worn out, and Harry could smell the drink on her breath. She sat next to him, slumped against his shoulder, listening while Norman told some yarn about travelling by bullock cart in India. They had to sleep out on deserted railway stations, Norman said, and in the morning, if you weren't careful, monkeys leapt down from the rafters, stealing your breakfast out of your hand.

According to Norman, the Tamil women gave their babies opium to keep them quiet, the tiny amounts scraped underneath a fingernail.

'They're black as coal, Tamil women,' he said. 'Have beautiful eyes.'

When he'd stopped talking, everybody was quiet.

Mac was smoking one of his cigars.

In one of the change kiosks, Les was arranging coins in enormous towers, building them up until they collapsed into the wooden till.

Sheila was filing her nails.

Without looking up, Elaine told them she was pregnant.

The baby was nearly five months.

She said she didn't know the father.

Norman seemed frantic. He got up and walked to the end of the fairground, then came back and shouted at her about being a tart. Sheila told him to shut his mouth, but Elaine said nothing, not defending herself, sitting on the waltzer steps, listening while Norman ranted. He went bright red. Getting up nervously, Mac took his arm and smiled towards Elaine.

'Leave her alone, Norman.'

To everybody's horror, Norman was crying.

'She should know better,' he yelled, rubbing furiously at his eyes.

'It's not the lass's fault.'

'Who's bloody fault is it then?'

'It's nobody's fault,' Elaine said quietly.

Calming down, Norman sat on the steps of the waltzer and let his hands rest between his knees. He stared stiffly out of the fairground, his mouth twitching. His eyes looked dreadful.

'You can't bring a child up on your own,' he said.

'I'm going to have to,' Elaine laughed.

'Plenty do,' Sheila nodded.

'You can't,' Norman told her.

When he asked her to marry him, she laughed in his face, and then said she would, as if it was a joke.

Norman told her he was being serious.

'Course you are,' Sheila croaked.

They got married in the local registry office, and had the reception in a small room in the town hall. Mac bought them all their furniture, and Mildred rented them a two-bedroomed flat overlooking the sea for practically nothing.

'You can keep your job,' she told Elaine. 'No need to live in.'

Harry went to the registry office with Arthur, who was home for his first turnaround. They sat at the back of the bare room and listened while the registrar read out the ceremony, then they walked together to the town hall.

'You look thinner,' Harry said, glad to see his friend.

'Fitter, you mean.'

'All that gutting.'

'Too fucking right.'

Arthur's hands were already scarred, a couple of white cuts where the gutting knife had gone in.

'It's hard,' he said, showing Harry how you had to bend

178

to pick the fish from the pounds when you were gutting. A big wave could knock you over. 'Fucking hard. But look at the money.'

Opening his wallet, he showed Harry the wad of fresh notes.

'You don't get that easy,' he grinned.

At the reception, Harry was introduced to Elaine's parents. They hardly spoke. The father was a sullen, scraggy little man, with tough, wiry arms. The mother was huge and red-faced, clutching a bright green handbag.

'Let us wish them everything they want for themselves,' Mac said, giving the toast and blushing over the words.

He'd agreed to be Norman's best man, and stood by him awkwardly throughout the day, embarrassed by all the fuss, happier just sitting on his own smoking his cigars or having a glass of whisky.

'I'm going to tell him,' he hissed when Harry asked if Norman was still the Happiland bouncer.

'Well, do it then, Mac. You can't let him go on.'

'Shut up, will you?'

'Look at him this year. Sooner or later he's going to get himself killed.'

Mac gritted his teeth and peered furiously at Harry, then rushed off to the other end of the reception room to talk to Elaine's parents.

'I shall do you breakfast again,' Elaine said when she found Harry looking at the presents.

'Don't be soft.'

'I shall. When you go digging. It was lovely.'

'Yes.'

For the wedding, Norman wore a dark blue suit, but when the two of them got changed to catch the train for Scarborough, he had on his grey cavalry-twill trousers, a new blazer with silver buttons, and one of the Jane ties, showing a picture of a naked girl, hand-painted on red silk.

Elaine gave Harry a wet kiss before she climbed into the car.

As they drove off to the station, Norman waved, and gave them a big grin.

Walking back along the promenade with Mac, Harry told him that he was going to try and get a job down on the docks.

'They sometimes take casuals,' he said. 'If I can get something without a card.'

'You'll still get your papers,' Mac said.

'Not if I'm living somewhere else.'

'Don't be soft, Harry.'

'I don't want to leave the town.'

'You'll have to, if that's what you're going to do.'

'No.'

'Same as Clive.'

'I'm not the same as Clive.'

When they reached Happiland, he spent the afternoon doing maintenance on the dodgems, and then helped Mac check all the locks on the windows and shutters.

At five o'clock, he went home to get his tea.

The house was empty.

He got the kettle going and then turned it off, grabbing his duffel coat and walking up past the cinema to Ted & Blue's.

There was a queue already waiting.

Twenty-nine

The woman showed him into a small room, not unlike a doctor's waiting-room, except that all the magazines on the table seemed to be about fish packing and frozen foods.

'You can wait in here,' she said. 'Mr Lunsett won't be long. He's just talking to somebody on the 'phone.'

Sitting down, Harry thanked her and glanced at the magazines on the table. A thick layer of dust covered the magazines and ashtrays as if nobody ever used the room. The woman stood at the door, checking her wristwatch against the clock over the gas fire.

'I'm Mr Lunsett's secretary,' she told Harry with a brief smile, making the wristwatch comfortable on her wrist.

Harry thanked her again. When she'd gone, he looked at the clock over the fireplace. Eleven-fifteen, so he was in plenty of time.

'Be early, but not too early,' his mother had told him. 'Create the right impression.'

Harry sat forward on the edge of his chair and looked at the magazines and leaflets on the table.

'A career in food packing,' one of the pamphlets said. There was a picture of a fisherman on the cover. He picked the pamphlet up and read the advertisement. 'With hard work and application, you can have an interesting career in this rapidly expanding industry.' He put the pamphlet back on the table and stared out of the grimy windows.

Walking along the promenade that morning for the interview, he'd stopped to listen to the buoy at the estuary. It rang intermittently, as though something had gone wrong with the timer, a hollow, clanging sound, drifting across the sea. The lighthouse glinted in the watery sun, and a trawler waited for the next tide just beyond the estuary mouth, motionless in the autumn sun. If the buoy was ringing, then fog must be coming in from the sea, but there was no sign of it.

At the tideline, a man was digging for bait, and a dog ran in great circles across the sands, barking stupidly at the gulls. Harry leant against the promenade railings and watched the man. He wished he could take his shoes off and go and join him at the tideline, digging into the firm ground. The sand would be wet and cold, hurting your feet. He could hear the sound of the spade as it went into the sand, squelching into the water just below the surface.

He looked at the pamphlet again.

The fisherman on the cover had a long beard and shining blue eyes. The oilskins he was wearing were years out of date, the kind you saw in films or old photographs. He was holding a fish Harry couldn't identify.

He tried to remember what his father looked like. A short man, with thick arms and huge hands. He said you needed quick fingers to work on the trawlers, gutting the fish. He never got further than a deckhand. It was hard work, eighteen hours at a stretch, hauling the nets in and gutting the fish. Off Iceland, the cold was sometimes so bad men lost their fingers from frostbite. That, or from carelessness, their hands so cold they didn't feel the gutting knife going in.

Harry remembered his father talking about the *Newton*, a trawler that had gone down off Iceland. A radio message came over that the *Newton* was heading into a northerly gale. Other ships in the area managed to get to shelter at Ritter Rook, but the *Newton* kept going. She was a modern ship, with all the latest equipment. By midmorning she was in bad freezing conditions which made it too dangerous to turn, so she continued dodging into the wind, hoping the mixture of high winds and low temperatures wouldn't last. But the winds continued flinging spray over the sides until she was heavily coated in ice. In gales like that, it was dangerous to get up on deck to clear the ice, and by the following morning the skipper was having difficulty keeping her head up into the gale.

It was the radio reports that his father remembered, the details passed around by the Sparks on his own trawler.

'Weather very bad, having to go full speed to keep up in the wind, continuous snow and freezing.'

That was the first one.

And a few hours later: 'Boat deck solid with frozen snow. Lads digging it out since breakfast. Terrible lot on bridge top and they're going up there at daylight if possible.'

The daylight was already gone on the early afternoon of the following day when *Newton* called again.

'Calling all ships,' she said. 'We are now taking heavy water.'

At 16.30 she reported: 'Aerials now icing up. Will call from time to time.'

At 16.45: 'Can anyone take a bearing on us on this frequency?'

One of the sheltering trawlers replied: 'Bearing as near as we can say NE.'

At 16.50 *Newton* called: 'Come to us. Position becoming serious now.'

The *Gainsborough* replied: 'We are coming to you, we are coming to you.'

At 17.04 *Newton* radioed: 'Going further over. No visibility. Still going over to starboard.'

At 17.05: 'Still going over to starboard, cannot get her back.'

At 17.08: 'Still going over, going over.'

'*Newton* going over' was reported in morse code for a further three minutes after 17.09, and then transmission ceased.

Harry's father had known many of the crew.

Harry listened to the story, sitting by the fire. A wind was howling outside. His mother was next door and his grandfather had gone down to his club on the docks.

'Why'd you go back, Dad?' Harry asked.

His father laughed abruptly.

Harry could remember the night, the storm beating against the windows. It was the storm that had made his father tell him. Afterwards, in bed, Harry listened to the rain battering against the window and imagined himself in one of the trawlers. He kept hearing the words of the sinking trawler.

'Going over, going over.'

And then the silence when the transmission ceased.

'Kelam?'

A man stood in the doorway of the waiting-room. He was smoking a pipe, sucking it noisily and banging it against his teeth. He held his hand out to Harry.

'You are Harry Kelam, I take it?' he grinned.

It seemed to be some sort of joke, and the man laughed loudly as he led the way through to an office where he told Harry to sit down.

'I'm Mr Lunsett. I understand from my secretary that you're applying for the freezer job we've been advertising. That right? Good. Well, the job's straightforward enough. You'll be working with Mr Sargeant in Freezer Eight. We provide boots, overcoats, headgear and gloves, but I should wear some pretty warm clothes as well if I was you. You'll be working in the freezer most of the day and conditions are pretty grim down there I can tell you. You'll be glad to get back in the sun, eh?'

Again the man laughed vigorously. His thick lips clenched around the pipe, flecks of tobacco all over his tweed jacket. Stretched taut across his stomach, his shirt buttons were straining as he laughed, black hairs straggling through the gaps. He leant forward and taking a form from one of the trays on his desk pushed it across to Harry and handed him a pen.

'When can you start, Kelam?'

'Monday morning.'

'Good lad. Well, you fill the form in and report to Gate Fourteen on Monday morning, seven-thirty sharp. Ask for Dave Sargeant, he'll look after you. The office will sort your cards out. First job, eh? You'll be very happy with Eskimo Foods, long as you work hard. Does your mum buy our fish-fingers, eh? That's the ticket.'

Outside, in the secretary's office, Harry stared at the form. He filled it in and handed it to her.

She read through the details briefly.

'You haven't put your national insurance number,' she said.

'I don't have one.'

'You'll have to get a card,' the woman said brusquely. 'We can sort that out Monday morning.'

Harry listened to her, standing in front of the desk and big typewriter. As she spoke she looked down at the letter she was typing as if waiting for him to go. He could see the small bald patch on top of her head, the skin through the thin hair patchy and red.

'Do you need a national insurance number?' he said, waiting for her to look up.

The woman sighed and took a file from the tray on her left.

'Didn't you read the advert? You answered it.'

Harry thanked her and made his way out of the building.

It was right on the main quay, and as he made his way back towards the exit gates a gang of lumpers were unloading one of the trawlers at the fish market. Men laughed and shouted above the noise of the winches lowering the fish baskets from the trawler, and Harry could see the filleters standing to one side waiting to start work. He stopped for several minutes, watching the men work quickly and noisily, the filleters smoking and fooling around as they waited for the kits of fish to be emptied on to the tables ready for filleting. During the summer months, it was a good job, but in winter, when the fish were frozen solid and cold winds blew off the sea straight through the fish market, it was hard work, standing in the cold for hours on end, dipping your arms in hot water to keep them warm. In the cold, the lumpers had the best job, keeping warm as they unloaded the catch, then clearing off to drink tea in the dock cafés.

Leaving the docks, Harry walked slowly along the sands and back to the promenade. It was warm out on the sands, and there were people about now, watching the sea, exercising dogs. The tide was coming in rapidly, and the trawler at the estuary was getting up steam, thick black smoke pouring out as she moved slowly towards the main channel. Harry sat down on one of the groynes and watched the trawler turning towards the river-mouth. Soon, it would be steaming for the lockpit, and the lumpers would begin unloading.

Getting up, he walked down to the tideline where the sand was hard and wet. The man digging for bait had already gone, but he could see the heaps of sand where he'd been digging. Slowly, the huge holes were filling with water. A slight wind had lifted off the sea and the buoy was no longer ringing, promising a clear afternoon. He could spend the afternoon on the fairgrounds, helping Mac on the big dipper or checking the balances on the fruit machines. In the evening, he might go to the Regal. They were showing *Rock Around the Clock* again. It was the second time that year.